Praise for *Shadow Weaver*

★ "[Connolly's] use of language and suspense is captivating, resulting in a gripping tale that is wholly original. Dark, yet dazzling, this first installment in a planned duology is sure to be popular. A perfect choice for fans of Kelly Barnhill's *The Girl Who Drank the Moon*."

—*Booklist*, Starred Review

★ "*Shadow Weaver* is a spooky thriller filled with danger and magic... A fresh take on magic and friendship not to be missed."

—*Shelf Awareness*, Starred Review

"Fans of *Serafina and the Black Cloak* (2015) will find much the same chills and sequel-primed mystery here."

—*Kirkus Reviews*

"Vivid and invigorating."

—*School Library Journal*

"Connolly's narrative is full of meaningful moral lessons—on the limits of loyalty, the importance of honesty, and the absolute necessity of trusting others... An enchanting new juvenile fantasy series."

—*Foreword Reviews*

"This book contains plenty of action and intrigue to keep the reader turning pages. It is quick to read and contains enough unsolved mysteries to make the reader look forward to the next title in the series."

—School Library Connection

"The theme of friendship is handled deftly here... A gripping finale reveals the truth about the 'cure' for magic, and readers will eagerly anticipate learning more in a promised sequel."

—Bulletin of the Center for Children's Books

Praise for *Comet Rising*

★ "Connolly again spins a magical tale; she deftly crafts moods and creates a sense of urgency that will leave readers breathless. The conclusion to the duology brings a feeling of relief, but a few puzzling questions remain, leaving the door ajar for future adventures, should Connolly choose to return to Emmeline's world."

—Booklist, Starred Review

Praise for *Hollow Dolls*

"Connolly...introduces new characters and a gripping plot with a twist–all sure to captivate readers."

–Booklist

"This fantasy covers a lot of ground–suspense, friendship, bravery, family, and magic. Plot twists will surprise even readers paying close attention... A recommended purchase."

–School Library Journal

Also by MarcyKate Connolly

Hollow Dolls duology
Hollow Dolls
Lost Island

Shadow Weaver duology
Shadow Weaver
Comet Rising

Dan Haring and MarcyKate Connolly
The Star Shepherd

A Breath of Mischief

A Breath of Mischief

MarcyKate Connolly

sourcebooks
young readers

Published by Sourcebooks Young Readers, an imprint of Sourcebooks
P.O. Box 4410, Naperville, Illinois 60567-4410
(630) 961-3900
sourcebooks.com

Cataloging-in-Publication Data is on file with the Library of Congress.

This product conforms to all applicable CPSC and CPSIA standards.

Source of Production: Versa Press, East Peoria, Illinois, USA
Date of Production: October 2022
Run Number: 5027919

Printed and bound in the United States of America.
VP 10 9 8 7 6 5 4 3 2 1

For my favorite mischief makers, Logan and Xavier.

CHAPTER 1

ALL MY LIFE I'VE LIVED WITH THE WIND. I WAS SWADDLED in blankets with threads woven from clouds, and when I cried, the Wind would pelt the earth with a rainstorm to lull me sleep. The birds and flying beasts in the castle aviary became my friends and companions, while the Wind scoured the lands, as was their duty. But the Wind always came home at a moment's notice if I needed them. All I had to do was ring a little silver bell, and soon a breeze would wash over me, and I'd know they were there.

The Wind claims me as their daughter, their windling, heir to their estate in the clouds. There is nowhere I'd rather be. We float over the earth, the little villages passing below us, the people as tiny as ants. Sometimes the Wind lets me stir the rain clouds until they spill over, and once, to my breathless delight, they even let me throw a lightning bolt.

The world below is interesting to be sure, but I've watched it all unfold from above, seen more than ever would've been possible if I lived on the ground. We've traveled far and wide as our cloud castle floats along over every part of the world. I know every river and mountain like the back of my hand. Besides, the Wind is a collector. On their journeys, they always find fascinating books and baubles, something new to amuse me and my companions. I suspect our library is unrivaled by any other in the whole world.

In short, I love it here. And today I get to do one of my favorite things—fly on the back of my gryphling companion, Gwyn. She's still young like me. The Wind brought her home to our aviary two years ago after she was injured in an attack by humans on her parents' nest. We nursed her back to health and have been inseparable ever since. She has the body of a lion and the head, neck, front legs, and wings of a golden eagle. When the sun strikes her feathers and fur, they glimmer like precious metal.

Today we soar around the high ocean cliffs, Gwyn occasionally dipping her toes in the water. I laugh at the salty sea spray. The Wind joins in the fun, blowing so hard that waves crest higher and higher and crash pleasingly against the rocky red cliffs. Our castle floats on a large cloud high above, and many of the birds from the aviary dash into the water to catch fish and soar on the wild winds.

"I wish the dragons were here," Gwyn says wistfully. "They'd love this."

Sometimes the larger flying beasts like rocs and dragons come to visit—they all know the Wind well—but it has been a long time since we've seen the dragons. They had shimmering blue wings and scales as hard and shiny as diamonds. But one night, a young dragon had a bad dream and accidentally toasted a couple of the other flying creatures, and they haven't been back since.

"They would!" I agree. "Maybe we can ask the Wind if we can visit them since they won't come to us."

"Yes!" Gwyn chirps. When she settles on the top of the cliff, we watch the Wind send the waves into a frothing frenzy, water hitting the rocks hard enough that we can feel the rumble under our feet.

A sudden urge overcomes me. I flash a grin at Gwyn. "Catch me," I say.

Then I leap off the cliff.

"Aria!" Gwyn grumbles as she takes off after me.

She knows I won't fall headlong like others might. I am a windling, after all.

Instead, I float.

I can't fly like the birds, but I drift down slowly, never worrying that I'll crash. The air is where I belong.

When Gwyn swoops beneath me, I grasp her neck feathers and seat myself on her back again. The Wind, watching all the while, laughs, and it echoes back to us. I send a smile and a wave into the sky.

"I hate it when you do that," Gwyn says.

"I know, but it's just so much fun," I say.

"You know, someday I may not catch you. Then what will you do?" Her feathers are ruffled now, but I try to smooth them over.

"I will be fine. I'll float down and maybe grab on to an edge of the cliff. Besides, the Wind is here. They'd never let anything happen to me. I'm always safe."

Gwyn shakes her head and doesn't say anything else. She flies me back to the cliff—this time a much safer distance from the edge. The Wind joins us, whirling up the red sand to briefly take on a swirling, smiling humanlike form.

"Let us go home," the Wind says. And we do.

⟲≈⟳

Later that evening, as the wind chimes that hang in the aviary tinkle sleepily throughout the house, I settle into my hammock.

The Wind brushes a kiss gently across my forehead. "Good night, Aria," they whisper.

"Good night, Wind. Will you sing me to sleep?"

The Wind whirls a bit of cloud puff into a smile—one that appears to be laughing. "You are getting old for lullabies," they say.

"But I love lullabies," I respond. "Yours always help me fall asleep."

"Someday, you will grow up, and you will not need me anymore, not even for my music."

"But I'll still want to hear it," I say.

"Then how can I say no?" the Wind asks.

The song begins as it usually does: mournful yet sweet, almost a howl to the moon and a whisper in my ear. Then it rises in tempo and tone until it ends on a peaceful chord.

"Good night, Aria," the Wind says again, then disappears into the clouds below. "I'm being called to the west. Tomorrow I must fly away, but I will see you again soon."

I can't help thinking that the timbre of the Wind's voice is a bit strange. It seems sadder than usual. But the Wind has already whisked themself away, so I make a mental note to ask them later, then let my heavy eyelids fall and pull me into slumber.

CHAPTER 2

IT'S MUCH QUIETER THAN USUAL WHEN I WAKE, BUT IT always is while the Wind is away. The wind chimes still make a pleasant melody that can be heard throughout our little aerial realm. Gwyn and I peer over the edge of the cloud, watching the village below as we float along. The village is flanked by a thick forest, and the treetops hop with birds. The people below move about their daily lives with no idea they're being watched. Sometimes we hover over the same village long enough to get a sense of the personalities inside it, but usually we only see them as we drift along, all the faces blending into one another. We've seen this village before. I recognize the mother and her young twin sons playing in the yard of a house on the outskirts. She's hanging laundry to dry while they play beneath her, jumping to reach the clothing that flutters in the breeze. One of the little boys yanks the leg of a pair of pants too hard, and the whole clothesline comes down. The mother scolds them while trying to hold in a laugh.

I snicker and so does Gwyn.

The gryphling sighs next to me. "Do you ever wonder what it would be like to remain in one place, Aria?" she asks.

I wrinkle my nose. "Goodness, no. The world is so big. The fact we get to travel is a gift. If we stayed in a village like the one below, we'd never see the rest of the world." I shake my head. "Or can you imagine traveling by foot? Walking everywhere would take ages!"

Gwyn chirps approvingly. "That's true. Flying is much more efficient."

"And fun," I say, rubbing a hand over her neck feathers.

When the village disappears from view, we return to the castle and greet our friends in the aviary. While most birds make their nests in the trees below, many choose to visit the cloud castle's aviary for companionship they can't find elsewhere. Since she's part bird herself, Gwyn particularly enjoys talking with them. I nestle into some pillows in one corner of the aviary and curl up with a book while listening to their chatter. I may not be able to understand regular birds, but Gwyn is special. Her kind is magical, and I suppose, as a windling, I'm somewhat magical too.

My hair is very pale and has a faint bluish tinge. So does my skin in the right light. Try as I might to keep it in check, my hair always seems to be moving as if wind rustles through it. And my bones are featherlight, which is why I can float instead of dropping like a rock.

The birds are normal animals and thus only visiting. Gwyn and I are permanent residents. Gwyn never talks about her family, and I've never wanted to pry, but when she arrived here, she was old enough that she should've remembered them. I'm not entirely sure where I came from, to be honest. I've always been the Wind's, and there is no doubt in my mind that I belong here and only here. The Wind and Gwyn and our delightful visitors are all the family I require.

But Gwyn's question still circles my brain. Why would I wish to leave the cloud castle anyway? Where else can I find a palace to call my own? Crafted of the finest, softest, yet sturdiest clouds, it has high turrets and winding halls, a library filled with the books the Wind brings me as gifts, and even a blooming greenhouse, watered by the rain before it falls to the earth. Not to mention the aviary and the castle grounds, with walkways through gardens filled with sweet little flowers that only bloom on clouds like ours, never seen by human eyes. Between the paths and flower beds, statues made from gray storm clouds stand tall, only holding their shape by the will of the Wind.

It's a paradise and it is mine.

"Aria," Gwyn calls, gesturing with her beak that I should join her and a black crow who is perched on one of the aviary's branches. "Come here."

I go to her side. She looks concerned. "What is it?" I ask.

"This crow has the strangest tale." The crow squawks in confirmation. "He says he came here because he wanted to see if the Wind was all right."

I laugh. "Of course the Wind is fine. Why wouldn't they be?"

"Well, the crow was nesting in the woods to the north when there was a sudden torrential downpour. Lightning, thunder, floods. Then, a few minutes later, it ended just as suddenly."

I frown. "That is odd. But the Wind may have decided a storm didn't strike their fancy any longer." I shrug. "They do change their mind frequently."

The crow squawks again, flapping his wings. Gwyn tilts her head. "I suppose that's true. Still, rather odd behavior. The crow said he'd never seen anything like it."

I smile at the crow and run a hand over his shiny black feathers. "Thank you for coming all this way and sharing your story with us. That was kind of you."

The bird preens, and I return to my cushions and my book, promptly forgetting all about the exchange.

In the middle of the night, I wake unexpectedly. It takes me a few moments to realize no loud noise woke me. Instead, it's the utter lack of sound that must have pulled me from my slumber.

The soft chimes that always tinkle in the breeze and fill the castle with music have stopped playing. A strange, uncomfortable feeling washes over me, but I brush it off. There are days when the wind lulls here and there. This must be one of those times. I'm sure the chimes will sing again in the morning as the breeze returns to push the castle in a new direction. It always does and it always will.

The Wind is the one constant in my life. I have no reason to believe that will ever change.

CHAPTER 3

GWYN'S PANICKED SQUAWKING YANKS ME FROM SLEEP IN the morning. She usually spends the night in the aviary where she's more comfortable, but this morning she's in the hall right outside my door.

"Aria! Come quick!"

I rub my eyes and open my cloud-white door in my pajamas. "What's the matter?" I ask.

"Get on and I'll show you."

I swing my leg over her back and throw my arms around her neck. Gwyn wastes no time taking off down the hall, but she can't spread her wings to their full width inside. Once we pass through the front door of the castle, she skids to a stop.

I gasp, unable to believe my eyes.

Instead of our usual dawn-filled view of morning, grass and hills roll before us as far as the eye can see.

The Wind's castle is on the ground.

I'm speechless, but Gwyn certainly is not.

"It must've happened while we slept. I don't understand how. But that's not all that's wrong with the castle. Do you hear it?" Gwyn's golden eyes stare intensely at me.

"Hear what?" I ask, unable to process that we're no longer soaring above the earth. My skin tingles, and I can't help wondering if I'm still dreaming.

"Exactly," she says, and her feathers stick out from her neck.

At my confusion, she sighs. "The chimes. They're gone." She points a claw at the castle. "The chimes that hung in the aviary are missing."

Horror flashes over me in a wave of heat. "Last night...I woke up because it was too quiet. I couldn't hear the chimes, but I chalked it up to a lull in the wind."

"That was no lull. Someone stole them right from under our noses." Gwyn glares in the direction of the aviary as if that might give the culprit a change of heart.

"How could they possibly be stolen? Only birds and flying beasts could ever hope to reach our castle." I frown. "Besides, what would anyone want our wind chimes for?"

"What are we going to do?" Gwyn flaps her wings. "We must get the castle airborne again!"

"I don't know that we can on our own. But I know who can help." I reach into my pocket and pull out my little silver bell. The Wind gave it to me long ago and told me that if I ever needed them and they weren't home, I could ring it once and they'd return immediately. I've only used it once or twice, but I always carry it with me—just in case.

I unhook the clapper and ring the bell.

It chimes pleasingly. But the Wind does not appear.

"Maybe it's broken? Ring it again," Gwyn suggests.

I ring it a second time. Still no Wind.

That same strange feeling from last night comes over me again. I don't like it at all.

"It's supposed to work. It always works," I say, a little out of breath.

"Well, it isn't working today," Gwyn says gloomily.

I stare at the bell and then at a nearby tree. Something looks odd about the tree. A terrible thought strikes me.

"Gwyn, could you take me up over the forest beyond the hills? I need to see something."

I climb onto her back, and we fly as fast as we can to the woods. The gryphling circles over the tops of the trees while I gaze down, feeling dizzy.

"What do you see?" she asks. "It looks like a regular forest to me."

"There's no wind. None. Not a single leaf moves below us."

Gwyn squawks mournfully in response. Then she takes us back down to the castle. When I dismount, I notice something else: I no longer float! I didn't realize it when we first left the castle, but now that the situation is sinking in, it's clear something is very wrong.

"I can't float, Gwyn," I tell her, almost in tears. My friend examines me carefully with her beady golden eyes.

"Your hair. It's not rustling anymore either. It's...flat."

I run my hand through my hair as if that could change anything.

"The Wind...the Wind is gone," I say.

I can hardly believe the words, but it's the only reasonable explanation. Something terrible has befallen the Wind. My parent, my protector. They left their castle in my charge, but I failed them.

"We must find out what happened. Maybe the Wind is hurt and needs help."

Gwyn tilts her head at me. "The Wind? Hurt? I've never heard of such a thing."

"I've never heard of all trace of the Wind vanishing either, so it seems the impossible is probable today."

Gwyn and I circle the castle. It's very strange for the structure of fluffy white clouds to be stuck on the ground. Even the statues in the garden have unraveled without the Wind to hold their shape. A fog hangs over everything today and shows no sign of lifting. The mist makes Gwyn's feathers slick and dampens my hair and clothes.

"Maybe we can try to give it a push to get it back in the air?" I suggest. We try our hardest at each corner, but the cloud castle is surprisingly heavy and determined to remain grounded. We're lucky it settled while we were floating over the plains and didn't get tangled in a forest canopy instead.

We spend the rest of the morning examining every inch of the castle, hoping for some clue or hint for how to return it to the sky where it belongs. Every so often, I ring my little silver bell, hoping against hope that the Wind just didn't hear it the first twenty times. But it's no use. The Wind does not return, and we come up empty-handed in our hunt.

We're eating lunch in the kitchen when we hear shouting outside. My blood runs cold.

"Someone's found the castle," I say. We race back to the entryway and peek outside. Humans—men—are wandering through the cloud garden and stomping all over the sweet flowers that grow there.

"We must get rid of them," Gwyn growls.

"There's more of them than there are of us," I say.

"I can peck their eyes out, scratch them with my talons," Gwyn says helpfully as she brandishes her claws.

"They're curious. We shouldn't hurt them," I say. "But we could scare them away." An idea begins to form in the back of my brain. "Why don't you go to the aviary and tell the birds we're going to need their help..."

Setting our plan in motion, Gwyn flies off, and I take a deep breath, steeling myself to step outside and face the men. I've only spoken to humans once or twice before. I open the front doors to the castle, and they swing wide, catching the attention of the men. I'm not very tall, but I pull myself up as much as possible.

"Greetings. For what reason do you trespass on my domain?" I try to emulate the Wind when their voice is big and booming, but instead it comes out sounding a bit odd. It doesn't have the desired effect on the group either. Most gawk, and a few of them laugh.

"Your domain?" asks one of the men, who steps forward. "This castle belongs to you? Or did you find it and want a place to play?"

I scowl at him. "I live here. You're ruining the front garden. We would appreciate it if you would leave."

He steps closer again, and this time the rest of the group follows suit. "Who is *we*?"

"Me and my family," I say. At my cue, Gwyn and all the birds in the aviary—more than a hundred—swarm from all sides of the castle, diving at the men. They duck and cry out as the birds fly closer and closer, and the ones who notice my majestic gryphling friend gawk before ducking and running too. Soon the birds have chased them all back into the woods, hopefully scurrying home to whatever village they came from.

I breathe out a sigh of relief, but my chest still feels tight.

We may have scared them away this time, but I've read enough books, seen enough scenes play out in villages as we pass, to know the nature of men. They will return. Next time there will be more of them, and they will be better prepared to fight.

CHAPTER 4

WHEN GWYN RETURNS TO MY SIDE, SHE PREENS WITH GLEE. "Serves them right," she says.

"They'll come back, you know. We can't stay here. It isn't safe."

"But we can't abandon our home!" Gwyn chirps. "It isn't fair."

I shake my head. "I agree, but we can't hold them off for long. They weren't prepared this time, but next time they will be. The only way we can protect our home is to get it off the ground, and we can't do that without the Wind." I straighten my spine. "We need to find them."

"But we don't know where they went," Gwyn says.

"I do. Before they left, the Wind told me they were being called to the west. That's where we'll start."

I quickly pack up provisions to last a while and not spoil, as well as some extra clothes, my favorite blue cloak, and a map of the realm from the castle's library. Then we head out in the afternoon before the men can return with reinforcements.

We take off into the air, passing a sparkling blue pond with children from the nearest village splashing in it not far from Cloud Castle. They're closer than I'd like, but there is no help for it.

We're wary of flying for too long. Gwyn is only a gryphling, after all, and with my full pack, the load is heavier than usual, and she tires faster. We fly as far as she can—well past the plains and over a mountain—then settle in a marshy area to give her wings a break.

We continue traveling by foot. It's strange, having to walk everywhere and not float when I please. Gwyn doesn't seem to like it much either. The ground is oddly squishy in places, and mud soon coats my shoes and her hind paws and fore claws. She *tsks* in distaste.

"Is this what humans do all the time? How unpleasant," she mutters.

"No wonder they'd rather live in our cloud castle," I say.

It's warm here too, and it isn't long before my hair is plastered to my face with sweat and the bugs buzz around our heads. I'm growing better at picking out which places are squishy and which are solid, and that helps us make more—and less messy—progress. After an hour of trudging, we find ourselves on firmer ground at the edge of great plains dotted with rolling hills.

"This looks much more inviting," I say. The long grasses and flowers bend slightly, but no breeze whistles through them as it should. My heart sinks in my chest. The Wind really is absent. But where could they have gone that they'd disappear so thoroughly? As far as I know, no one can kill the Wind. They must be in trouble of some kind.

And we must help them.

"Did you see? The grass didn't budge an inch when I flapped my wings," Gwyn says. "It only moves when we push it over." She flicks a claw at a nearby blade of grass.

"Everything is so still. It feels like the world is frozen." I shiver. The sooner we can find the Wind and get back to normal, the better.

"We're headed west, but are you sure we're on the right path? How can we even tell?" Gwyn asks.

I knit my brow. "Birds," I say. "Can you ask the nearest birds what direction they last saw the Wind blow? We can use them to keep us heading in the right direction, I think."

"Good idea." Gwyn launches into the sky then swoops to land on a hill where a flock of birds forages for food. She chirps back and forth with them, and the birds dance excitedly on their

legs. Her appearance may be fearsome, but Gwyn is a social creature. She's always happiest when others visit to tell her interesting news and stories of the world. I suppose I am too.

Soon Gwyn returns and shares what she learned. "They
said the last time they felt the Wind, they were heading westward. Then, they turned north. Not long after, every hint of a
breeze disappeared."

"North?" I mull it over. "I suppose they *do* change their mind
often. Still, it seems odd. They said the west was calling to them.
It sounded as if they had something to do there. They made no
mention of the north."

Gwyn shrugs. "It's worth a look. Climb on."

I shoulder the pack with our supplies and get on her back
again now that she's rested her wings, and we take off into the
northern sky. We fly for some time, but when the sun begins to
dip below the horizon, we decide to set down near a river for the
evening. There's a willow tree not far from the bank, and we
curl up under its long fronds. I can't help staring at them as I fall
asleep. There's something terribly sad about a willow tree that
can't even sway in the breeze. It makes my heart ache.

I've always known the Wind mattered to me, but I don't
think I recognized how they impacted the world around me in
so many little ways, from my own ability to float to how they
made the trees dance. I miss the Wind, their presence replaced

by a hollow spot in my chest. I close my eyes, wishing they were here and singing me lullabies again.

༄

I wake to the feeling of being watched. I bolt upright, waking Gwyn in the process.

"What's—"

"Shhhh!" I hiss.

The gryphling tilts her head, curious.

I hold still, only my eyes moving to take in everything within my line of vision. I suck my breath in sharply when I see it.

There, between the reeds at the riverbank, is a pair of bright, clear blue eyes in a boy's face. His hair is wet and dark brown but with a sheen of blue and green when the light hits it. He stares at us as if we're the two strangest things he's ever seen in his life. When he sees I've spied him, he rises to his feet with a slightly guilty expression on his face. He appears to have been in the water, but somehow his clothes are dry. When he steps toward us warily, I realize there are slits in his neck that flare and contract as he breathes. Gills.

"What are you?" we both say at the same time. I laugh, but he takes a step back and frowns.

"I'm Aria. I'm a windling," I offer. "This is Gwyn, my best friend and a gryphling. We won't hurt you, I promise."

"A windling? What are you doing all the way down here? I thought you lived in the sky."

Now it's my turn to be surprised. I didn't think anyone knew much about me or the Wind. "We did. But the Wind is missing. Haven't you noticed? Not even this willow moves unless it's pushed by someone's hand." I flick a nearby frond in demonstration.

"Oh. I just thought it was a lull."

"No, definitely not a lull," I say with my hands on my hips.

"Then that sounds quite bad."

"It is. That's why we're here. We're seeking the Wind. We think they must be in trouble, and we need to find them so we can help."

"I see." The boy casts around for a moment as if he's lost something. Perhaps only his train of thought.

"What's your name?" I ask, slightly exasperated by this nameless boy with gills.

"Oh, my name is Bay. I'm a waterling."

"Heir to Water," I murmur. I knew there were otherlings, but I never met them. I did see a fireling once, but that was a long time ago and only for a moment. Gwyn is still convinced I imagined it though.

"Exactly. That's why I have gills." Bay puts a hand to his neck. "I live in the water too. Our castle is down there." He glances at his feet. "I'm sorry the Wind is lost. I don't know what I'd do if the Water disappeared like that."

"Is the Water here?" Gwyn asks curiously.

Bay shakes his head. "No, they're with the tides in the eastern oceans. But if I need them, I can call them using this shell." He pulls a pretty little shell from his pocket, all pale pink with golden ridges.

"Like my bell," I say to Gwyn, and she nods. I turn back to the boy. "Did you happen to notice which way the Wind went the last time they passed through here?"

"I'm sorry, I wasn't paying attention. But I'll keep an eye out in case they come back."

"Thanks," I say. "It was nice to meet you."

Bay smiles broadly. "Yeah. It was." He looks over his shoulder at the water for a moment then back to us. "Hey, do you two need breakfast? I was going to make some for myself with lizard eggs and berries."

Gwyn practically drools, and I laugh. "We do, and we can share our bread with you too, if you like."

He beams and sets about making a small fire in a cleared part of the riverbank and cooking his eggs. I produce some of our bread and toast it beside him.

"I've never met another otherling before," Bay confesses. "I'm the only waterling. I can talk to the fish, but they never stick around for long. Usually, the only one who keeps me company is Nixi, and he comes and goes as he pleases."

I wrinkle my nose. "What's a Nixi?"

A splashing noise comes from behind Bay.

"Oh, he's here now. He was hiding. He's shy." Bay gestures to the rippling water encouragingly. "Come out and say hello, Nixi."

The water burbles, then an enormous creature breaks through the surface, its spindly legs gripping the edge of the bank. My mouth drops open so fast, I nearly lose the bite of toast I'm chewing. The creature is paddle shaped with a hard, orange-colored shell covering its entire body. Several sets of legs and two sets of pincers stick out from its sides, while its beady eyes take us in.

It's at least two feet taller than Bay, but the boy pats the thing's shell without any sign of fear. "See? We're friends."

"It's—it's nice to meet you, Nixi," I stammer. Gwyn, for once, is actually speechless.

Nixi doesn't appear to have words either. The creature makes a clicking sound and smashes his pincers together.

"That's how he says hello," Bay reassures us.

The creature waves one leg then sinks back into the water.

"See? He can't stay above water for too long. We have the most fun when we swim together. Do you swim?"

"I confess, I've never needed to swim," I say. I could always float up and away. Now…swimming might be necessary.

"I swim," Gwyn says. "I can keep Aria safe in water if need be."

"Oh, well, I could teach you sometime, Aria. If you wanted," Bay offers. "It's really quite simple, and fun, once you get the hang of it."

I smile. "Do you need gills to do it right?"

He blushes. "No, but it doesn't hurt."

I laugh. "Then I'd love to learn the next time I'm here."

Bay grins. "Swimming is the best. Sometimes the Water tells me stories when they're around."

"Stories?" Gwyn's ears perk.

"Oh yes," he says. "They always bring back interesting stories from their journeys."

"The Wind does that too," I say. "But they collect books and trinkets they think I might like."

"Tell us a story," Gwyn says. "One of your favorites."

A light shines in Bay's eyes. "Have you heard the one about the princess who was swallowed by a giant oyster?"

Gwyn chirps. "She became the world's most precious pearl!"

"What about the brothers who were turned into swans?"

Gwyn nods impatiently. "Yes, yes. You must know something we haven't heard yet."

"Oh! Do you know the one about the otherling who couldn't choose?"

"No!" Gwyn gasps. "You must tell us."

I lean into Gwyn's golden feathers while Bay relays the tale.

"Once, a very long time ago, there was an otherling raised by the Wind."

"They were a windling too?" I interrupt.

"Sort of," Bay says. "He was raised by the Wind for the first part of his life. But when he was twelve, the Wind found him gazing longingly at the ocean as they passed overhead. 'Do you wish to swim in the ocean?' the Wind asked the windling. The windling shook his head. 'No, I wish to live in it. Breathe the water as the waterlings do.' At this, the Wind was troubled, for their charge was a windling, and they loved him dearly. For the next few days, the Wind did everything they could to show the windling how wonderful it was to be a windling. But every day, his response was the same: 'I wish to live in the water as the waterlings do.'"

"Finally, the Wind could no longer bear to see their child so miserable, and they visited the Water. 'Water,' the Wind said, 'Please, will you make my windling happy and make him your waterling?' The Water agreed and soon grew to love him as their own. But one day, the Water found the new waterling sitting on the beach of an island longingly gazing at the forest on the mainland. 'What is the matter?' asked the Water. The waterling replied, 'I wish to walk through the forests, feel the moss under my feet, and commune with the green things that grow like the earthlings do.' The Water was very troubled by the waterling's words, and over the next several days, the Water tried everything they could to show him the magic of being a waterling. But it was to no avail. The waterling's longing for the forests would not be overcome."

"So, like the Wind before them, the Water went to the Earth and begged them to take the waterling and make him an earthling so he would be happy. The Earth agreed and soon grew to love him as their own. The new earthling was happy for a time, but then one day, the Earth found him gazing longingly at a fire ravaging one of their forests. 'My earthling, you must leave here, or you will be burned,' the Earth said. The earthling replied, 'But of all the things I've seen, I love the Fire best. I wish to walk through the warmth of the flames unburnt, swim in a volcano's lava pools, and never be cold again.' Now the Earth was deeply troubled by the earthling's words. Indeed, they began to suspect he might have set the forest fire just so he could watch it."

"With a heavy heart, the Earth went to the Fire and asked them to make the earthling a fireling so he would finally be happy. The Fire agreed, and the new fireling joined them in their volcanic palace. Finally, the otherling was happy. But his happiness only lasted for one year. The fireling, now a mature otherling, went to the Fire and made a request: 'I can't be just a fireling, or a windling, or a waterling, or an earthling. When I am one, I envy the others. Please, I must be all of them at once.' The Fire was very surprised by the fireling's request. 'My child, I love you like my own, but I cannot grant your request. It is impossible.' The fireling was grieved at this. 'Then I shall never be truly happy,' he said."

"Every day for the next month, the otherling came to the Fire with the same request, and every time, the Fire had no choice but to deny it. So the fireling left and went to make his plea to the Wind. Though it pained them to deny the boy anything, the Wind could not fulfill his request either. The fireling journeyed to the Water and the Earth and made his case to them as well but was met with the same response. Cast down, the otherling returned home to the Fire and begged them to make him all the otherlings at once one final time."

"'My child,' said the Fire. 'I would never deny you anything I could grant, but this is the one thing I cannot. There is no power in the world that can make that true.' And the fireling responded, 'Then make me none of those things, because it is too much to have one if I can't have them all.' The Fire was grieved to hear this, but the fireling was adamant. So the Fire made him a simple human, and the boy went on his way."

"What happened to the boy?" Gwyn asks, her usually beady eyes as round as saucers.

Bay shrugs. "No one knows. He was never heard from again."

"He must have regretted his choice eventually. What a selfish boy!" I say. "I can't imagine ever giving up the Wind. I mean, Water is lovely and all, but it isn't for me."

Bay smiles at me. "I feel the same about the Wind. It's wonderful! But Water is my home."

"Do you know any other good stories?" Gwyn asks, but I give her a stern look.

"I'm afraid we ought to be going. Our mission is rather urgent." I stand and rub the dirt from my trousers.

Bay stands too, running a hand through his strangely colored hair. "Of course. If I see the Wind, I'll let them know you're looking for them."

"Thanks," I say. "And thank you for sharing your breakfast and your story with us." Gwyn bows low, showing her gratitude as well.

We bid Bay goodbye, then keep heading north. Gwyn consults with birds every so often, and occasionally we veer west again, only to be pulled back in a northerly direction. It's almost as if the Wind was trying to fly west but was pulled off course.

But what could do that to the Wind?

We follow the Wind's trail for two more days, growing

more and more puzzled by the hour. Then, finally, the trail goes cold, and we find ourselves at the edge of a deep, dark forest.

And blocking our path is an immense wall of briars.

CHAPTER 5

I PEER THROUGH THE PRICKLING THORNS AND CAN JUST make out a wall of bricks. "I think there's something behind there," I say.

"Well, there's only one way around this obstacle, and it isn't through," Gwyn says. I climb on her back, and she takes off, grazing the brambles. She hisses as tiny beads of blood appear on her flank.

"A bit too close," I say. "I have some bandages in my pack. I'll patch that up when we're on the ground again."

She soars upward, higher and higher, until we clear the massive tangled briars. Beyond them is a large estate.

The estate sits on a hill overlooking the woods and the wall of briars concealing it. A line of trees edges the property where the briars end. We set down near the trees and hide in the shadows between them, unsure whether it's safe to show ourselves. If something could stop the Wind from blowing, what could it do to us?

"I say we fly over the mansion and scope it out first," Gwyn says, and I don't have a better plan. I don't know what I expected to find when we set out after the Wind, but it wasn't this.

"We'll have to be careful and swift and on the lookout for traps, even in the air."

Gwyn takes off again, and I grip my hands in her neck feathers. I feel certain this is where the Wind must be, but I can't understand why or how. In fact, I feel lighter now than I have in days. That could mean the Wind is nearby and their magic is lending itself to me again as it always has before.

The thought is both encouraging and frightening.

Gwyn takes us up and over the grand estate. It's a long, wide brick building, with a huge dome-like structure in the center. There are no windows in the dome; it's just shiny metal, glimmering in the late-afternoon sun. Something about it makes my gut clench.

Past the briars and tree line, the rest of the estate is strange too. Once, it must have been fine and well tended, but it has fallen into disrepair. An aging brick wall surrounds the mansion, slowly being devoured by ivy and crumbling to dust in some parts. The gardens are wild and overgrown with weeds choking out what plants initially lived there. In the few places where there's wood on the exterior of the mansion, the paint is worn and chipped. I half expect some wild thing to race out to confront us as we trespass from the air.

Nothing comes. No hint of life yet. I can't help thinking it must be a trick. Or a trap.

Convinced we're alone, Gwyn finally alights on the back lawn of the estate. Really, it's more of a field. The long grasses rival any we saw on the plains the other day. With my heart in my throat, I tiptoe toward the house with Gwyn, staying as low to the ground as possible. As a gryphling, Gwyn is rather good at this—her hind half was made to prowl through long grass just like this. It's a little trickier for me, but I make it work as best I can. It feels like it takes an eternity to reach the decaying black wooden door at the back of the house. It was probably once a servants' entrance that's fallen into disuse.

"Do you think anyone lives here?" Gwyn asks.

"It's hard to tell," I say. "Perhaps it's abandoned and inside is something dangerous and old that did...something to the Wind."

I still can't quite fathom what could stop the Wind. But my imagination is on fire with possibilities.

We push away moss and ivy to reveal the slimy, dirt-coated handle. I turn it, and the whole handle comes off in my hand.

"You broke the house!" Gwyn chirps.

"I didn't mean to!" I say, tossing the handle to the ground and wiping my hands on my trousers. There's a dark hole where the handle was before. "Do you think you can pry it open with your claws?"

Gwyn shrugs but pushes forward and threads a claw through the hole, then she yanks with all her might. Something metal clatters on the other side. Then the door gives way, sending us both flying backward. With panicked breaths, we remain still and tangled together on the ground for a full minute, just to be sure we didn't wake anything inside the house. No other sounds follow, so we dust the cobwebs and ivy off ourselves.

"Are you ready?" I ask Gwyn. She nods curtly, and we step into the mansion.

It's dark and dank, but some light filters in through the windows. It takes a few moments for our eyes to adjust. Once they do, we find ourselves in an old kitchen. Rusted pots and pans hang from the ceiling, but there are some vegetables in a basket by the far door.

My breath catches in my throat. "Someone still lives here."

Gwyn scowls at the basket while she sniffs it. "Yes, those are definitely fresh. Strange. Look, here's some bread too." She points to a shelf I hadn't noticed where two loaves of bread lie out.

"It must not be many people. There isn't that much food," I say, wrinkling my nose. I can't imagine cooking or eating in such a dirty kitchen, but then, humans may be stranger than I thought.

We leave the kitchen behind and explore the house. Dust and yellowing linens cover most everything, but we can make out the shapes of tables and chairs and sofas beneath them. There are statues and tapestries along the walls, and scenic paintings too. If the mansion had been kept up, it would be quite lovely.

It isn't long before we find ourselves in front of a strange, shiny metal door. It's clearly the newest thing in this house.

"This doorway must lead into that dome," I murmur, and Gwyn chirps quietly next to me.

"Perhaps the Wind is trapped in there and can't find a way out since there're no windows," she suggests.

"Perhaps," I say. Uneasiness prickles up my spine.

To my surprise, the door opens easily. Whoever lives here must expect potential visitors to be deterred by the briars. They're probably correct. I just happen to have a secret weapon in Gwyn and her wings.

We step through the door and stop in our tracks. Inside the dome is an enormous room. And inside the room is an enormous machine. We walk around it, marveling.

"What in the clouds is this?" asks Gwyn.

The strange machine is all metal tubes and twisting wires, with bulbs of glass here and there. We make our way to the back of the machine, and that's when we see it: a huge glass bubble.

Inside it is a whirling mass—of Wind.

My heart leaps and quails at the very same time.

"Wind! Can you hear—"

"Who are you? What are you doing in my laboratory?" barks a man who appears in the doorway.

He does not seem at all happy to find us here.

CHAPTER 6

"WE'RE—WE'RE HERE FOR THE WIND. THEY'RE TRAPPED IN your machine," I say, trying to keep the quiver from my voice.

"Let them out of that bubble!" Gwyn squawks.

The man smiles. "The Wind isn't trapped in the bubble. They're helping me." I'm surprised he seems to have understood Gwyn. Humans normally can't understand creatures of magic like her.

"Helping you?" I frown deeply as an odd feeling worms its way through my stomach. The Wind can be a kind, helpful soul, but I've never heard them speak of a man like this, or a wild estate, or a strange machine. Besides, the man doesn't look special enough to be worthy of the Wind's help. His hair is a mousy brown, and the only striking feature about him is his eyes. I can't tell what color they are, and it almost seems to shift as he moves toward us. Around his neck hangs an odd-looking key on a black cord.

"Oh yes," the man says. "My name is Worton, and I brought the Wind here because I need them." He moves into the room and pats one of the metal pipes on his machine. "The machine will solve everything."

"What do you need the Wind for? What does this machine do exactly?" Something about this man is familiar, but that feeling in my gut tells me not to trust him. Gwyn growls next to me. We circle the machine at the same speed as Worton; neither of us wants to let him get too close in case he tries to capture us too.

"Why, the Wind is a key part of what powers this machine," he says. "What is more powerful than the Wind after all?"

What indeed. But it still doesn't explain anything.

"My machine, once completed, will bring harmony to the world. There is so much strife, but it will solve everything."

"I don't trust him, Aria," Gwyn says. "This machine doesn't look like an answer; it looks like a very confusing question."

"I agree," I whisper. Then, to Worton: "How did you get the Wind into that glass bubble? And how can we get them out? I'm the Wind's daughter, and I came here to rescue them."

Worton's eyes widen at this. "Oh, you're a windling. That does explain your gryphling companion." He puts a hand on his chin, considering. "Well, it's simple really. I explained to the Wind what I was trying to do, and they agreed to help. I found the design for this machine in an old grimoire in the tomb of an ancient warlock in a petrified tree. Long ago, the witches and warlocks understood how to balance the world. But the world has gone off-kilter and must be set right. The Wind understood and got into my machine willingly."

"Willingly?" My chest feels tight and itchy. I can't believe my only parent and protector would choose to leave me with no warning. But I also don't have an alternate explanation. I don't see how a simple man like Worton, even with a grimoire, could force the Wind into these tubes and bubbles against their will.

"But *we* need the Wind more. All the wind has disappeared from the lands. Haven't you noticed?"

Worton shrugs. "Not at all. It is never very windy in this region anyway."

"Even our home, our castle in the clouds, has settled on the earth without the Wind to keep it in the sky where it belongs. There's no breeze to toss the ocean waves, to rustle leaves on the trees, to spread seeds throughout the lands and make the green things grow. The world feels like it's standing still. We need the Wind back."

"I am sorry." Worton makes a pitying face. "But I need the Wind more. My work is too important to stop now."

"Please, if the Wind only knew what difficulties their absence has caused, I'm sure they would agree with me. You said the Wind entered your machine willingly."

I clench my hands in frustration. I can see the Wind, and they can see me, but Worton is in the way, preventing me from getting close enough to speak to them.

The man raises an eyebrow. "I disagree. I think they'd tell you to be patient. And to return home."

Ire rises in my chest, filling me so quickly, it feels like I might explode. "I have no home without the Wind! Men have overrun our castle, and the Wind is my only family. Please, let me speak to them."

Worton sighs. "I'm afraid it's impossible to speak to the Wind inside the machine. But in the spirit of the witches of old, I will give you a chance to free the Wind. If you complete three challenges before the moon wanes, I will deem you worthier than me to hold the Wind in your hands."

Gwyn's eyes narrow at the man, but I place a warning hand on her wing. Worton may not believe we're equal to his challenges, whatever they may be, but he also doesn't know us. I am determined to prove him wrong.

I hold out my hand to shake on it. "You have a bargain," I say. Gwyn sighs and makes a *tsk* sound in the back of her beak.

Worton raises his brow. "Don't you want to hear what the challenges are first?"

"Of course, but I'm willing to take them on regardless."

Somehow his smile grows wider. I refuse to let that deter me.

"The first is to find and retrieve a chalice that is never empty. The second is to obtain a candle that can penetrate any darkness and never burns out. And the third is to find the purest and most brilliant diamond in the world."

Gwyn scowls at his words, but I ignore her. "Is that all?"

This time Worton does indeed laugh. "Yes, that is all."

"What do you want with them, anyway?" Gwyn asks.

Worton smiles. "They're valuable. Who wouldn't want them?" He shrugs. "Really, it's a test of your worthiness."

He turns to the cluttered worktable that stands near the great machine and flips through an old, heavy book; then he scribbles something on a small sheet of parchment.

"Since I'm feeling generous, I'll even give you a clue." He hands me the parchment. "Here is all the information known about the whereabouts of these fabled objects."

The chalice lies west in a watery grave.
The candle burns bright in a silent place.
The diamond is buried where no man can trace.

I read the clues carefully then nod. "We accept the challenge. We shall return before the moon completely wanes."

With that, Gwyn and I depart, trailed by bursts of the man's laughter.

"What are you thinking?" Gwyn asks as soon as we're out of earshot. "We can't find these things! They're legends! And we only have a week until the deadline!"

"Many legends are real—why not these too?" I counter.

"Oh, I have no doubt they're real and very well hidden. And very well guarded." She shakes her head and snaps her beak. "It's a fool's errand. You should have just let me peck his eyes out."

"I doubt that would have gotten the result we desire," I say, smirking.

"Well, it would have made me feel a lot better," she grumbles. "The poor Wind. Caught in that globe. I don't believe for a second that they're helping him willingly. I can't imagine how that man captured the Wind though. It shouldn't be possible."

Sadness washes over me again. It was horrible to see my only parent trapped helplessly like that. "It shouldn't be, but it is. Now we must fix it. The world needs the Wind."

"So do we," Gwyn says.

"And so do we," I agree.

At Gwyn's signal, I climb onto her back, and she takes off into the air, soaring over the wall and the briars. We head in the direction of the first clue, but all our fears and hopes remain behind, trapped in a glass bubble alongside the swirling, captive Wind.

CHAPTER 7

WE FLY STRAIGHT ON A WESTWARD COURSE. I CAN'T HELP wondering what drew the Wind this way in the first place. Gwyn and I both feel sure it wasn't Worton. Maybe we'll discover what it was on our adventure; maybe we'll never know.

What we do know is that we must complete our quest for the three strange items. The Wind has always been there for me. They chose *me* as their windling. I can't fail them.

"What should we be looking for, do you think?" Gwyn asks. I'm as puzzled as she is by the vague riddle. Occasionally we pass over a village with a cemetery on the outskirts, the graves marked by gray slab tombstones. But none of them would qualify as watery like in the riddle.

"Let's fly west until we can't go any farther," I say with a shrug. "Hopefully there will be some kind of a sign." I memorized the brief poem, and I repeat it to myself while leaning into Gwyn's feathered back. "The chalice lies west in a watery grave…"

"Do you think Bay could help us find it?" she wonders aloud.

"Maybe, but I don't wish to trouble him. We could be searching a long time for these things." I let out a weary sigh.

Gwyn squawks. "Not too long, I hope. We only have a week to free the Wind."

We fly onward, the lack of wind below us still unsettling. From above, it feels as though the world is holding its breath. Waiting for the Wind, who might never return if we fail.

An uncomfortable knot forms in my throat; failure is unthinkable. The Wind is vast and grand and strong. It isn't right for them to be confined to such a small space. The world needs the Wind, and the Wind needs the world.

When it grows dark, Gwyn sets us down in a forest not far from the coast, and I take out some matches I packed and make a quick fire while she goes off to hunt. By the time she returns, the fire crackles, and we have a dinner of roasted rabbit.

"I've been thinking about the poem," I say, drawing my cloak around me. "It must mean the chalice is somewhere near the ocean."

Gwyn chews thoughtfully. "That would make sense. But

how will we determine where exactly? The coastline surrounds the entire continent!" Her feathers fluff, but I smooth them down.

"We know it must be west, so that limits it to the western coastline."

"Which is still miles and miles. What if the watery grave means it's deep underwater? We'll never reach it."

My heart sinks. I hadn't thought of that. "We have to try our best. If we can't figure it out, then we move on to the next item. We have no time to waste, and we can always circle back later."

"And enlist Bay's help too."

"Yes, if it comes to that, we likely will need his help. I don't see how we could retrieve the chalice on our own if it's deep beneath the waves. So let's hope it's not."

We settle down to sleep, and I lean against Gwyn's warm, soft feathers. I don't want to be discouraged when we've barely begun the hunt, but a hard lump of tension has already formed in the pit of my stomach. I may have put on a brave face for Worton when I accepted this challenge, but doubt nibbles at my toes. These tasks are daunting and overwhelming. But I am the daughter of the Wind; who else can save them? I do my best to think positive thoughts as sleep finally overtakes me.

◦⥾◦

The next morning, the sun greets us, and we hastily eat leftovers for breakfast, then get on our way. We fly until the ocean comes into view. We've seen it many times before and played in the sea spray, buoyed up on the wings of the wind. But while the tides still roll in and out, there is no wind to tease the water, to rile it up into a frothing frenzy. The endlessness of the ocean takes on a very different feel without the safety of our cloud castle to return to at a moment's notice.

"Why don't we fly down the coastline and see if we can find any clues?" I suggest. Gwyn squawks her approval.

The sun is high over our heads, making the breezeless day hot and sticky. I tuck my cloak in my pack, grateful that my shirt and trousers are made from a soft, gauzy material. The coastline—sometimes rocky, sometimes sandy—stretches for miles and miles before us. Gwyn flies for as long as she can, but after our first pass up and down the coast, she has no choice but to alight on the beach. We've been pushing her limits, and flying is more physically exhausting without the wind currents to glide on.

As the Wind's heir, I can't help feeling responsible for all the airborne creatures in my parent's absence. But if we fail to free the Wind, who will take care of me? What will become of me and Gwyn? Will I still be a windling? It's all I've ever known; I can't imagine never being able to float again or never feeling the breeze gently rustling my hair.

I swallow the sick feeling rising in my throat. Then I slide off Gwyn's back and give her a few minutes to rest, taking off my shoes to dig my toes in the inviting sand. It makes me feel a little bit lighter and helps clear the circling heavy thoughts. We didn't see anything that looked like a watery grave on our flight, save the ocean itself, but I'm certain there must be a clue. I just need to focus on the task at hand.

"Have something to eat," I say, passing Gwyn some of the leftover rabbit. Our packs are a little lighter than they were when we set out, but with Gwyn hunting to supplement our food, they should last us another week. "Then we can walk down the beach. Maybe we need to be closer to the water to see what we're missing from above."

Gwyn sighs glumly. "Aria, what if...what if Worton only gave us this quest because he knew it was impossible?"

I stiffen. I refuse to believe that could be the case, even though I wouldn't put it past Worton. Something in his eyes made him seem untrustworthy.

"Nothing's impossible. Why, a few days ago, we thought it was impossible for the Wind to be captured; now here we are." I shake my head. "No, even if this quest is a trick, we can't give up. If Worton can trap the Wind, then we can find a way to free them."

Gwyn chirps in response, and when she finishes her snack,

we head back out on foot. Waves lap at our toes as we wander down the beach. The sand glitters in the sun, but the water is cold and biting. We walk for a long time, over dunes and hills, through tide pools, and out onto outcroppings and seawalls, hoping for something, anything, to hint where the chalice might be hiding. By the end of the afternoon, our feet are exhausted and dirty, and our spirits have sunk as low as the ocean floor.

Nothing. No hint of a chalice. Or its watery grave.

"We're missing something," I grumble.

"It's impossible," Gwyn laments. "I'm done with walking. Let's fly back to our campsite and try again tomorrow."

I'm grateful for the break and climb onto her back. She takes off, and this time we soar over the ocean instead of following the curving line of the coast. It's a more direct route that will return us to our campsite faster.

I scowl at the beach and rocky parts of the shore dotted with patches of seaweed and shells now that the tide is low. Our defeat has shaken me more than I wish to admit to Gwyn.

Then I sit up straighter. "Gwyn!" I shout. "Circle back toward that cliff."

She gives me a puzzled squawk but does as I ask. My heart thrums in my chest as we draw closer.

The base of the broad cliff, now revealed by the retreating tide, is riddled with holes—caves. Some are small, but one looks big enough for Gwyn and me to walk through without having to hunch over.

"See that cave, there in the center?" I say to my companion. "Can you land near there?"

"Hold on," Gwyn says.

Hope soars within me. "Nowadays, humans dig graves in the ground, but long ago, they buried their dead in caves." Or at least that's what my books have told me.

"A watery grave," Gwyn says as understanding dawns.

"Yes! Maybe. Definitely worth checking out."

She flies straight for the largest opening, then lands in the wet sand a few yards away.

The cave opening is a few feet off the ground, but Gwyn gives me a boost, and I tumble inside, landing on the slick rock.

"Aria!" Gwyn cries, flying up and helping me to my feet. "Are you all right?"

"Yes, I'm fine." Then I grin. "Let's explore."

The cave floor is very slippery. It must be completely underwater when the tide is in. No wonder we didn't see it before. Lucky for us, it's low tide now. We follow the winding passage into the cliff, and darkness envelops us completely.

"Do you have any matches?" Gwyn asks. I search my pockets and manage to find the ones I tucked away last night when I made our fire. I strike one, and it lends us enough light to see a couple feet in front of us but no farther. I don't know how long we walk. It could be minutes or miles—but it's slow going nonetheless.

Then the darkness seems to lift a little, almost as if there's light up ahead. When the passage opens into a cavern, we understand why.

A beam of light shines down from above. There's a hole in the top of the cliff! A basin stands in the center of the cavern. Curious, we approach the basin.

"What a strange place," Gwyn murmurs. The walls are worn smooth as sea glass, and shiny like it too. Clumps of seaweed cling to the entryway, and pearly shells of many colors line the walls and basin.

"It's beautiful," I say. "Though I wouldn't want to be here when the tide comes in."

She nods her agreement. "Let's hurry up before it does."

The basin is about three feet in diameter and perfectly rounded—it appears to have been carved from the rock rather than a natural formation. Water swirls inside, but it seems to be retreating into the center.

My breath catches when I spy a flash of silver in the water.

"Look!" I reach for the silver as the water vanishes inside it. Sure enough, it's a smaller bowl shape, though I see no obvious path for the water to have traveled through it. Gwyn has to hold me so I don't fall in, but I manage to reach far enough to get my fingers underneath the silver rim and yank it free.

I gasp as the chalice—a silver cup with a simple silver stem—comes loose in my hands. We tumble backward.

"This is it," I whisper. "This must be it." I turn the heavy cup over in my hands. It's perfectly crafted and smooth, not a single scratch despite the elements it's been exposed to for who knows how long.

"Did it take the water into itself?" Gwyn asks. "I thought that's what I saw."

"Yes, and that confirms this must be what we need." I throw my arms around her neck as relief fills me. "We found the first treasure!"

Gwyn embraces me back then glances anxiously toward the cave tunnel. "Then we should hurry to leave here. I heard a rumbling. I think the tide may be returning."

I carefully place the strangely dry chalice in my pack, and we hurry through the tunnel. We move as quickly as we can on the slippery rock by match light. Something rumbles in the distance, and water begins to trickle over our toes. Nervousness fills me, but we don't stop moving. I've never feared water before, but that was when I could float away.

Now that we're on our own and the gifts the Wind bestowed

on me have vanished, the world has become a much more dangerous place.

The rumbling soon turns into a roar, and the water rises to our ankles. Gwyn shivers and squawks. "It's cold, Aria. I don't like this."

"Me neither," I say, trying unsuccessfully to keep the tremble from my voice. "We have to keep moving. We must be halfway to the entrance by now."

But the water rises faster than we can move. The deeper it gets, the more it slows us down. Soon it's up to my waist, and we still can't see the light from the cave entrance.

"Aria…" Gwyn whines.

"I know, I know," I say. My breath stutters in my throat. I have no words to reassure her or myself. We found our prize, but at what cost?

"I wish we'd asked Bay to come with us," she whispers.

"Me too," I admit. My legs are freezing from the cold water. All I want is to see the sun again and feel its warmth.

When the water reaches my chest, fear clutches my heart. I can't stop shivering now and my feet feel like bricks. The water begins to get rougher, shoving us toward the walls and knocking us down. I slip and fall, gasping for air as I push my head back above the current.

It takes a moment for me to realize my pack, waterlogged as

it is, suddenly feels lighter. I flail around, and my hands light on a spare shirt and one of our waterskins floating nearby. My pack must have opened when I slipped. Hurriedly, I feel around the pack, and my heart nearly stops.

The chalice is gone.

"Gwyn! Keep going. The chalice is missing. I need to find it!"

She squawks something in response, but I don't hear most of it as I dive into the water. I can't see anything. All I can do is grope around the rocks and hope. The next few moments seem to stretch on forever.

Then my fingers bump into smooth metal.

I fumble with it then burst out of the water holding the chalice aloft.

"Aria!" Gwyn cries. I can just make out her form from the faint light now present in the tunnel. We must be farther along than I thought.

"I found it!" I grunt as I try to find my balance in the high water again. "Ugh! All I want is to be free of this stupid water!"

Then something strange happens.

The water stops rising. Impossibly, the current is drawn into the chalice. The cup should be full; instead, it takes in more. Faster and faster until all the water in the tunnel is gone.

Gwyn and I stare at each other in shock.

"How did you do *that*?" Gwyn asks.

"I have no idea," I say, breathless. "There's no doubt this is the treasure Worton wants. It must be able to give and take water at will."

"That could come in handy," Gwyn says. "Prettier than a waterskin too."

A shiver runs over my shoulders. I don't like the idea of giving the chalice to Worton, but it's a small price to pay if it means releasing the Wind.

I tip the cup upside down, just to be sure no water falls out. Then I place it back in my pack. A quick check reveals that our food stores are still all right. The bread was secure inside a leather packet, and a quick rinse in fresh water should make the fruit and vegetables I packed good as new.

"Let's not waste any more time in here," Gwyn says, and I agree. We continue, and the faint light grows brighter. Soon we reach the upper cave and the exit. Relief buzzes between us like a palpable thing when I step on the sands and Gwyn stretches her wings toward the sun.

The tide appears to have paused a foot or two from the cave entrance. Neither of us wishes to remain here while it comes back in again.

"Get on," Gwyn commands.

I climb onto her back, and we soar over the ocean again. Gwyn flies with the sunset behind us until we reach the forest where we camped the night before. Despite being weighed down by a heavy chalice, I feel lighter than I have since the Wind left.

The first quest was more dangerous than I'd anticipated, but we had a stroke of good luck today. I only hope our luck holds and we can find the other items in time to get the Wind back.

CHAPTER 8

I RISE EARLY THE NEXT MORNING, LETTING GWYN SLEEP. I start a small fire. I can't get the remaining clues out of my head.

> *The candle burns bright in a silent place.*
> *The diamond is buried where no man can trace.*

The chalice line at least had a direction—west—which proved useful. But the next two clues are much vaguer. I'm not sure what to make of them.

I'm still puzzling over it when Gwyn yawns and stretches. I pass her some breakfast, and she gobbles it up.

"Where should we head next?" Gwyn asks between bites.

I sigh. "I'm not sure." I throw up my hands. "I have no idea where to look for the candle. But maybe the diamond is in the deepest, darkest forest? It sounds like a place to get lost, which sort of matches the clue."

Gwyn shrugs. "Why not? We're on the outskirts of the largest stretch of forest in all the lands. We may as well start there and see what we can find."

We head deeper into the woods. The going is slow—there isn't much room for a beast such as a gryphling to fly here—but we search high and low, up trees, and under ferns. We peer into dark hollows and between craggy outcroppings. But we find no hint of a brilliant diamond or where one might present itself.

As the tree trunks become thicker and the branches hang down, brushing over our shoulders, we take a break for lunch. The forest floor is covered in dry, crunchy leaves, green moss, and soft ferns. Everything has a distinct earthy scent but not an unpleasant one. We can hardly see the sky between the branches above us, and it almost feels as if we're in another cave rather than a forest.

We don't talk much while we eat. Our packs are a little lighter than they were when we set out, but with Gwyn hunting to supplement our food, they should last us another week.

I've put away our food and risen to my feet when the shape of a boy peels off a nearby tree, startling Gwyn. His hair is brown with green at the tips, his eyes a dark brown, nearly black, and his skin tanned. But that begins to change as he moves away from the tree, almost as if the colors of his body can shift like a camouflage. By the time he stands before us, his skin is paler, and his eyes are a bright green. His hair has only a few hints of green left in it. His pants and tunic are a simple brown, but his cloak changes color in the light.

I know what he is. "You're an otherling too. An earthling," I say.

His eyes widen. "How did you know? And what do you mean *too*?"

"I'm a windling." I smile at first, but then it falters. At least I believe I'm still a windling. With the Wind gone, I'm not entirely sure about that anymore. But I don't know what else to call myself.

"Really?" he says, suddenly interested. "I've never seen one of you before."

"Nor I, one of you," I say. "But it's good to meet you. This is Gwyn, my gryphling friend. My name is Aria."

We shake hands. "I'm Terran. The trees are my friends." He gestures to the forest around him. Despite the lack of wind, the trees rustle in response to his words.

Gwyn squawks. "Trees aren't supposed to do that."

Terran laughs. "Well, you only think that because you don't know trees like I do. What brings you here? I thought windlings stayed in the clouds."

Gwyn and I exchange a glance. Part of me wants to tell Terran...but part of me is also uneasy about it. While Bay was very nice and Terran seems kind too, we don't really know them. And we can't afford anyone getting in the way of saving the Wind.

"We used to," I say carefully. "But the Wind has disappeared. We need to rescue them."

Terran's eyes widen. "I was wondering why the wind wasn't whistling through the trees as usual. That explains why the trees have been uneasy lately too."

"Yes, we must get them back. Otherwise, we'll never be able to return home to the sky."

Terran's face takes on an earnest expression. "I can't even imagine that. Do you know what happened to the Wind?"

I exchange another glance with Gwyn. "They're trapped. We're trying to find the means to free them."

Gwyn pipes up unexpectedly. "The Wind is trapped in a glass bubble that nothing can break, but it can be cut by a very special diamond."

She winks at me, but Terran doesn't notice. I admit, it's a clever way of finding out if he knows anything about the diamond. Though if he did, would he tell us? Would he help us?

Terran's brow furrows. "We do have diamonds in the earth. Maybe it's one of those?"

"It must be the purest, hardest diamond in existence," Gwyn says, clicking her beak. I know she means well and that we're desperate to free the Wind, but deceiving Terran, even with half-truths, makes me uneasy.

He bites his lip. "I do know of a special diamond, but it isn't mine to give. You'd have to ask the Earth."

"Where can we find them?" I ask. Perhaps Gwyn's way is a good idea after all.

"They're around but usually sleeping. I see them mostly as the seasons change. You can journey to their castle under the ground and wake them up." He frowns. "Be gentle about it though. I've never tried waking them before, and they may not like it. I can show you where the passage begins."

"Thank you," I say. "It would be helpful to have a guide. We don't really know where to start."

Terran glances around the forest longingly. "I can't go into the passage with you. I have duties as an earthling. I must take care of the forests. The trees need me. But you can tell the Earth I sent you."

"We'd be grateful if you can show us the passage."

He beams then gestures for us to follow him deeper into the woods. While we walk, he tells us of his time as an earthling, and I share what it's like to be a windling.

"I have lots of duties," he says. "The trees need care, you see.

Or they might get choked by vines—or worse, poisonous fungus—if left unattended. They need attention, someone to talk to them, or they'll wither up and die. I couldn't bear that. So, every day, I walk these woods, saying hello to all the trees and making sure they have what they need."

"That sounds like a lot of work," I say. "Being a windling isn't so hard. Mostly we float, and the Wind has been teaching me about making storms. That's awfully fun. Do you ever leave the forest?"

"Sometimes," he says, brushing aside a low-hanging branch then patting a moss-covered trunk. "I do like to wander fields, especially in the summer when all the flowers are blooming. And the mountains too. I've taken a few trips there to care for those trees, but they're heartier than the ones in the woods."

"Do you ever talk to the humans?" Gwyn wonders aloud.

Terran shudders. "Not if I can help it. The Earth warned me long ago that humans tend to take from the woods and not give back. I try to leave dead branches and sticks that make good kindling not far from the edges of the forest so they stay out of the older areas. I must protect them."

"That's smart of you. That way everyone gets what they need."

He smiles. "Exactly. The trees appreciate it too. They don't like humans wandering around the forest either."

The forest grows dark and the tree trunks thicker the deeper we move into the woods. The smell of the earth, warm and strange, fills my senses. Birds sing and insects hum, and other creatures tumble through the undergrowth. Ferns brush against our knees, and there is no discernible path that I can see, but Terran clearly knows the way. He doesn't pause; he keeps moving.

"I've never been in the forest like this," I say. "We've only flown over it before. I always admired how the leaves swayed in the wind and how lovely they are when the colors change in the fall, but I had no idea it was practically a realm of its own beneath the canopy. It's lovely here."

"I sure think so," Terran says, shyly running a hand through his dark hair.

We walk for a long time—the forest is vast and takes much longer to traverse by foot than the coast did by wing—and it is close to dark by the time we stop in a clearing. At the very center is a huge tree—bigger than any we've seen so far. Its branches stretch toward the sky. Thick vines encircle the limbs and hang down toward the ground. The trunk is about as thick as five grown men standing shoulder to shoulder, and the branches are larger than any of us below it. The other trees have given this one a wide berth, leaving a great circle between it and its nearest neighbor.

"I never knew trees could get this big," I breathe.

Terran grins. "I spend most of my nights up in these branches. It's very safe and offers excellent protection from the elements."

I tentatively touch one of the enormous leaves. "What a wonderful home you have," I say. Gwyn squawks approvingly.

"Why don't you camp here for the evening and then journey to the underside tomorrow?" Terran suggests. "It's a warm night, and I have plenty of food stores to share, if you'd like."

It is late, and I am rather hungry. I'm sure Gwyn is too. "Thank you, that would be lovely. It would be best for us to start our underground journey when we're not so tired. Should I make a fire?"

Terran gasps, his expression horrified. "Oh no. Not here. Fire terrifies the trees."

"Oh," I say, surprised. But of course, when I think about it, it makes sense. "How do you cook?" I frown.

"Cook what?" he asks. "I eat the fruits, nuts, and vegetables the Earth provides."

Gwyn's eyes narrow. "What about rabbits?"

"Ew, no. The rabbits are my friends too."

Gwyn harrumphs but says nothing else, which is a relief. I don't want to insult our new friend. I pat her feathers, and she whines slightly.

"I'll get us some dinner. Wait here," he says, gesturing to a circle of downed logs beneath one of the larger branches.

Terran scampers up into the tree, climbing as if he was born to do it.

"Don't worry," I say to Gwyn. "We'll get you some meat tomorrow. While we are in the Earth's domain, we need to honor their ways."

She grumbles but doesn't argue. Moments later, Terran reappears, his arms full of the promised food. We sit together and share the wealth. Gwyn discovers she loves fruit, and I taste vegetables I've never had before. To our surprise, when the food is gone, we're not at all hungry anymore.

"Let me show you where you can sleep," Terran says and leads us to a branch. He glances between us and the steep trunk and frowns.

"Don't worry, Gwyn can fly us up. Just tell her where to go," I say.

"It's the second branch up. There's a wide space where you can both sleep safely. Even if you were to roll over in your sleep, you wouldn't fall off. I promise."

I laugh. "I should hope not." Then I quickly sober. I've never worried about falling before. But now that I can't float...maybe I should be more concerned. Fear about what will happen to us if we can't free the Wind tries to creep in, but I shove it away.

If I let those worries in, it will send me into an unending spiral of doubt.

That would do nothing to help us complete our tasks. That's what I must focus on instead.

I get on Gwyn's back, and she takes us up to the right branch. Terran scrambles off to his own branch and waves good night while we settle in.

"Thank you for the hospitality," I say. Then Gwyn and I curl up together and fall asleep.

CHAPTER 9

WHEN WE WAKE IN THE MORNING, TERRAN HAS ALREADY gone, presumably off to fulfill his many duties as an earthling. But he did leave us some fruit and nuts that make a fine breakfast when combined with our bread and cheese.

Last night, he pointed out the hollow in the base of the great tree. According to Terran, it leads down into the depths and to the Earth.

And the diamond we need to free the Wind.

"Do you think the Earth will give us the diamond?" Gwyn asks as we eat.

"Honestly? No, I don't. The Earth doesn't know us. Why would they give us something so precious?" I shake my head.

Gwyn grows serious. "What if we don't ask? What if we search for the diamond instead?"

"You mean just take it?" I ask.

"That's what we did with the chalice. Why not this too? We can always return it later."

"Can we though? We don't know if this is really all a test or if Worton wants them for something. Besides, with the chalice, there wasn't anyone to ask."

"The quest seems like a test to me," Gwyn says. That was the impression I had too and what Worton claimed, but there's something about that man that makes me not trust him.

"You're probably right." Inside, I cringe. Borrowing the diamond without asking for permission would be a betrayal of Terran's trust. On the other hand, we can't free the Wind without the diamond...

"Let's see which we find first—the diamond or the Earth. If we find the Earth first, we ask permission to borrow it. If we find the diamond, then we mark the location, and we'll return it as soon as possible."

Gwyn squawks her approval. "Excellent plan."

We finish our breakfast, and Gwyn flies us back to the ground from our branch campsite. We approach the hollow of the tree with a small measure of trepidation. I feel confident that Terran wouldn't have directed us here if it weren't safe. But on the other hand, what is safe for earthlings isn't necessarily safe for windlings and gryphlings.

But we have no other options. With only a grumble or two from Gwyn, we walk through the hollow and follow a dark pathway that spirals down, down, down into the earth. The darkness envelops us, but soon our eyes begin to adjust, helped along by a glowing fungus that spreads over the walls.

"How far down do you think we'll have to go?" whispers Gwyn. It is so quiet underground that whispering seems the right thing to do.

"I don't know. 'The diamond is buried where no man can trace.' It might be quite far."

Gwyn chirps. "I don't like the sound of that. I never imagined questing would require spending so much time exploring strange tunnels!"

I pat her neck feathers soothingly. "Hopefully this will all be accomplished soon, and then the Wind will be back in their castle, just as they should be."

She huffs. "Soon would be nice."

The dark path winds downward, making our pace slower than I'd like. I belong outside, free to feel the sun on my face. Soon the fungus is joined on the walls by skeletal white roots and wiggling pinkish worms. Here and there, the edges of great boulders form part of the wall, and in other places, smaller stones poke out from the dirt. Shiny black beetles and more strange insects I cannot name scamper between our feet, off on their own journeys. It's lovely and creepy and a little scary all at the same time.

At first, it's cold beneath the earth, but then it begins to warm slightly. I don't know if I'm adjusting or it's really getting warmer, but I'll take it either way. Side passages begin to form, offshoots of the main tunnel, puzzling me and Gwyn.

"Should we follow one of those? What if the diamond is that way?" Gwyn worries.

I chew my lip. "I don't know. I think we should stick to the main tunnel. Terran didn't tell us to take any turns."

But soon the main tunnel splits into three directions. Perplexed, we stop and try to determine which is the best option.

"They all look the same to me," Gwyn says with a tremble in her voice. I place a hand on her neck and stroke her feathers, but I'm just as nervous. The tunnels are large enough for us to stand upright, but neither of us enjoys being underground. Our recent experience obtaining the chalice isn't helping matters either.

The deeper we go, the more it feels like a cold hand tightens around my chest.

"Let's try the passage on the right," I suggest. "But we have to be careful to remember each turn we take."

Gwyn swallows hard and bobs her head.

We start down the right-hand tunnel, but it isn't long before we're forced to stop. The passage continues, but it has narrowed to a point where we could only pass through by crawling. The thought of getting into a tight space like that so far underground—or worse, getting stuck there—is enough make bile rise in my throat.

"Let's try the one on the left instead," Gwyn says. I agree.

We retrace our steps and enter the left-hand passage. We continue for long enough that our bellies begin to grumble. It must be near lunchtime, and we pause for a quick meal. Gwyn is growing more nervous the deeper we get, her feathers sticking straight up from the back of her neck. My attempts to calm her are of no use.

"It can't be far now," I say reassuringly, but the tremor in my own voice gives away my fears.

She paws the dirt with one claw. "Let's move. The sooner we find this diamond, the sooner we can leave."

We attempt to keep to the single path, but offshoots appear every so often, and too many times, we're forced to choose a direction. Some narrow quickly, and others end in small caves, forcing us to double back and try again. I do my best to remember each turn, but it becomes more difficult with every one we add.

After the tenth time, Gwyn stops, visibly upset. Panic is brewing in my chest too, but I put on a brave face for her. As the Wind's heir, I'm responsible for the creatures of the air. Though

I fear I'm not doing a very good job of keeping Gwyn safe right now. Still, I'm grateful to have her with me. This quest would be much more terrifying without a companion.

"What do we do, Aria? I don't remember all the turns we took. It's too many!" she squawks.

A trickle of panic slides up my spine, but I set my jaw against it. "I remember enough of them. We're not lost yet. Our choice is between giving up and losing the Wind forever or continuing until we find what we need."

"But what if we can't find our way out? What if we never find the diamond?"

I shudder involuntarily. More than anything, I do not wish to get lost down here. But that's more than I can admit to Gwyn right now.

"We won't be stuck down here. Eventually either Terran or the Earth will find us and help us."

At least I hope they will. It's a gamble, but we're the only chance the Wind has.

Gwyn inhales deeply. "All right. Then we must continue."

After walking for what feels like another hour, our persistence is rewarded. The tunnel we're in ends, opening into an enormous cavern. We step into the cave, jaws slack. Above us, stalactites hang down, glowing like stars. It's almost like looking up at the night sky. From our vantage point, the path slopes down a hill, leading into a huge maze of stalagmites. They form row after row of intriguing patterns, all leading toward a small structure at the center with four columns and a roof.

"It's a labyrinth. 'Where no man can trace,'" I say.

"Indeed. No man could hope to get all the way down here. And if by some miracle they did, there's no way they could get to the center." Gwyn says.

"Luckily, we're not men. We're a windling and a gryphling." I grin at my friend.

She chirps a laugh. "That we are. I can get us over to that building quickly. Then we can get out of here," she says.

As I climb on her back, I notice an odd mound of dirt and rocks and grass—the latter of which surprises me most—encircling one side of the labyrinth. When Gwyn takes off, I get a better view, and I suck my breath in sharply.

It looks very much like a person, asleep on their side. The strange hilliness could easily be a head, shoulders, and hips, tapering off into legs and feet.

"Gwyn," I whisper in her ear. "I think we should be very quiet while we examine that structure."

She doesn't respond, but I can feel her curiosity beneath my hands on her neck.

The labyrinth is fascinating as we fly over it. All twists and turns doing an elaborate dance to confuse the poor souls who might dare to enter. I'm glad Gwyn has wings so we can avoid that challenge, but it's oddly pretty too, especially from above. Gwyn reaches the center and alights right before the columned structure. Without a word, I slide off her back, and we cautiously enter the building.

"What was it you saw from up there?" Gwyn whispers in my ear.

"I think...I think I saw the Earth." I frown. "Only I'm not sure. If it was them, they were asleep."

"It would be very rude to wake them," Gwyn says.

The building is dark at first, but it's crafted from a white stone, almost as if it were hollowed out and polished from a huge boulder. In the center is a pedestal piled with jewels. Some polished, some rough. Some of gold and silver, some of ruby and sapphire and emerald.

And many, many diamonds.

"This must be the right place, but how are we ever to figure out which diamond is the right one?" My heart quails at the sight. Worton must have sent us on this quest because he was certain we'd fail. Maybe he even tried to locate these items himself and had no luck. It was cruel to give us hope, only for it to slowly slip away.

I straighten my spine. I can't think like that. We found the chalice. We can find this diamond. There must be a trick to it.

Gwyn uses her beak to move some of the treasure around, no doubt hoping to see a diamond that stands out from the others. I frown at the pedestal. Then I walk in a circle around it. There are carvings in the white stone of the base. The first side seems to depict a face surrounded by flames. The next, a face blowing wind. Then, a face in the trunk of a tree. And lastly, waves swirling in the form of eyes and a mouth.

All four of the major elements.

This must be a clue. I examine them more closely, and Gwyn's long neck arches next to mine. Each is carved in the same style—set in a circle with a flourish beneath. I run a hand over the flourish, searching for any rent or seam. When I press the wind carving, something shifts inside the pedestal. Quickly, I move around the base, pressing in each carving, leaving the earth for last. When I press that one, the shifting sound grows louder, and a drawer shoots out from the top of the pedestal.

Gwyn gasps as I straighten up.

Resting in the little drawer is a diamond. It isn't any larger than the others, but something about it radiates significance. Reverently, I pick it up, and it sparkles in my hands under the glowing cavern lights. I can tell just by looking at it that it's clearer and purer than any of the other lovely gems in the pile.

"This must be it," I say. "It's perfect."

Awe and relief shine in Gwyn's eyes. "Yes, and that means we can leave."

I carefully place the diamond in my pack and then swing my legs over Gwyn's back. She wastes no time flying us to the cave's entrance. Something rumbles when we land. I swear the strange mounds shiver. Without a word, we rush back into the tunnels.

The trek to the surface is long and even more tiring than the journey down. Our path is all uphill. I feel much heavier than before, almost as if that diamond is weighing me down. Still, we move as quickly as we can. We don't even stop for a meal, despite the hunger gnawing at our bellies. We both feel an urgent need to get aboveground, so much so that it's hard to feel victorious even though we now have two of the treasures needed to free the Wind.

The fact the ground continues to rumble under our feet and I'm no longer certain we've taken all the right turns doesn't help one bit. When we reach a tunnel split where both sides result in dead ends, we're forced to stop.

"We're lost, aren't we, Aria?" Gwyn says, clawing the ground nervously.

"Yes," I say. "I'm sorry. I thought I could remember all the turns. But I must have taken us the wrong way accidentally." I sink to the ground. "I have no idea where we went wrong."

"Should we retrace our steps?" Gwyn suggests.

"I'm not sure that will help. It might get us even more lost," I say.

A wild look glints in her eyes. Suddenly, she begins clawing at the walls. "We'll dig our way out if we have to. I can't stand to be trapped underground any longer. We have to get out! We have to get out!"

I push to my feet and wrap my arms around Gwyn's body tightly until she stops clawing. When she finally calms, she rests her beak on my shoulder and whimpers.

"I'm sorry. I'm so sorry," I say. Tears burn in my eyes, blurring my vision. I brush them away and straighten up. "Let's retrace our steps like you suggested. At least that's productive."

We head back until we find the last place the paths diverged and take the other tunnel. This time I'm more keenly aware of my surroundings. All the tunnels are lined with the glowing fungus, but some are brighter than others. I think the first tunnel we took to get down here was one of the brighter ones. Maybe if we try to stick to whichever passage glows the most, it will lead us back.

We do our best to follow the glowing path, but it doesn't always work. Sometimes, both paths are dim. But whenever we can choose a brighter one, we do.

"There are a lot of beetles out now," Gwyn says as we find

the next glowing tunnel. "It's almost like they're marching somewhere."

She's right. Several shiny black beetles are also taking this tunnel, marching in a line with a foot or two between each one. Now that Gwyn mentions it, I've seen them in several of the brighter tunnels too.

My breath catches. "Maybe they're headed up to the surface."

Gwyn snorts. "I'm sure they know their way around the tunnels better than we do."

"Let's follow them. As long as we keep heading uphill and not back down, this might work."

We follow the beetles through the trembling tunnels until, at long last, we feel fresh air on our faces. We step out into the forest, relief washing over us like a cool balm. It's night now, and darkness hovers over the great tree. Terran may be slumbering above us in the branches, but we don't wish to disturb him if he is, even to thank him.

All we want is to leave.

The great tree shudders, shedding a few enormous leaves.

"We'll return it, I promise," I whisper to the tree, unable to shake a feeling of uneasiness. It must be lingering claustrophobia.

"Let's go, Aria," Gwyn says. "I feel like the trees are watching us."

"They may very well be," I say. "Terran considers them friends."

"I still don't like it," she says as I get on her back again.

It feels like eyes are on us as we find a clearing where Gwyn can take flight and break free of the forest. Almost like the trees' branches reach for us as we leave. As if they'd pull us back into the Earth's realm if they could. I swear the leaves shiver across the canopy—even without the Wind to rustle them.

I can't decide if it's my imagination or not. But I do know one thing for certain: the forest isn't happy at all.

CHAPTER 10

WE FLY UNTIL GWYN'S WINGS TIRE; THEN WE SET DOWN ON the plains and make camp beneath the stars far enough from the nearest town that no humans should trouble us tonight. We're both exhausted and unnerved by our harrowing experience in the realm of the Earth.

Hopefully our final task, finding the candle that never burns out, will go more smoothly. We only have a few more days before the moon vanishes from the sky.

"Did we...did we do something bad?" Gwyn asks as we drift off to sleep.

I bite my lip. I've been asking myself the same question. "I didn't think so at first...but now I'm not so sure." That uneasy feeling still clings to me, wrapped around the tight knot of worry for the caged Wind.

Sleep overtakes me at last, but not before I wonder, *What exactly has Worton sent us out here to do?*

⤾ఎ⤿

The next morning, we share breakfast from the remaining food stores in my pack and plan where to hunt for the candle.

"If we go south, there's a volcanic range," Gwyn says. "One of them is still active, or so I hear."

My eyes light up. "Yes, I believe the Wind told me once about the Fire holding court in a volcano. The candle can't be too far from there." It seems these treasures are near the seat of power for each element. I wonder if the castle where Bay grew up was near where we found the chalice. It probably was.

A hint of nausea tickles the back of my throat, but I swallow it down and finish my breakfast.

We have no other means of freeing the Wind from Worton's strange machine. There is no one to save them but us. What choice do we have? The world needs the Wind.

I dust a few crumbs off my trousers and then take out the diamond to examine it. The gemstone is astonishingly perfect in every way and surprisingly heavy. I hold it up to the light and sunbeams refract in all directions. It is so clear that I can see right through it, not a single trace of imperfection. Just staring at it takes over my senses, almost like falling into a bottomless well…

"Aria? Aria!" Gwyn says, knocking the diamond out of my hand. "I think we should put that away."

My mouth drops open; then I scramble to pick up the jewel. "Yes, right, of course. We need to find the...the..."

"The candle!" She snorts then scratches the dirt with her front claws. "Instead of preparing for our next quest, you've been gawking at that thing."

I give the diamond one last look and slide it into a pocket in my pack. I don't want it to fall out accidentally. What would we do then?

We set out in a straight line to the south. There is another dense forest and a lakes region between us and the volcanic range. We'll fly over the forest—we're not willing to enter another until we're ready to return the diamond—but will rest at the lakes, maybe make camp there depending on how much ground is left to cover and how exhausted Gwyn is from flying.

But first we walk so Gwyn can save her strength for later. We're not sure how large the forest is, and we don't want to have to land before we're clear of it. It isn't long before we hear a new sound echoing across the plains.

The thunderous sound of horses.

They're coming from a town not far from where we are. One that almost seems familiar, but it's hard to say for certain since I'm not accustomed to seeing towns and villages from this angle. Three men on horses appear to be heading right toward us.

"They aren't coming for *us*, are they?" Gwyn asks.

"I can't see why they would," I say.

"We should run, to be safe."

I agree and get on Gwyn's back. She takes off as the men draw near. They yell at us in angry voices, hands raised and pointing, but we're too high in the air to understand what they say.

I can't help feeling like we narrowly escaped.

The men were oddly familiar. I can't place where I've seen them before… But we're safe now and have left them far behind. They have no hope of catching up to us.

We don't risk alighting on the plains but continue flying to the south. When we reach the forest, Gwyn soars right over it. Flying is glorious. It feels like freedom. It would only be better if the Wind were here to tug at our hair and feathers and join the fun.

Soon. All we have to do is find the candle, return to Worton, and reclaim the Wind as ours. Then we can all go home.

I watch the trees pass beneath us. I don't think I'll ever get used to seeing them still. The rustling of the wind was so commonplace that its absence is jarring. I bet even the trees miss the Wind. The whole forest seems more listless today than yesterday. I'm not entirely sure, but it almost looks like the edges of the green leaves are beginning to brown even though it is still summer. The changing of the seasons and the colors of the leaves shouldn't happen for several months.

I chalk it up to mutual grief and don't give it another thought.

ᙍᘏᙓ

By midday we reach the lakes region, and good thing too because Gwyn is near exhaustion. We stop to rest for a longer-than-usual lunch so she can regain some of her energy. Flying without the Wind is taking its toll on her.

We're no longer in the woods, but there are patches of trees interspersed with smaller vegetation throughout the lake lands. It's lovely here. From above, deep-blue dots scatter across the landscape, some forming odd shapes, and others connecting here and there. We've chosen to have our lunch on the sandy strip of beach by a lake not far from a tree line. We rest on a few large rocks on the shore and share some bread and cheese. Gwyn keeps eyeing the lake.

"Do you think there are fish in there?" she asks.

"I'd expect so," I say.

She licks her beak as her belly rumbles. "I could go for a fish."

"Then fish you shall," I say with a laugh. I remain where I

am while she steps into the water. She is an excellent swimmer and paddles out, her eagle eyes examining the water with anticipation. She moves in lazy circles; then her neck shoots into the water and draws back carrying a prize: a wriggling silver fish.

She returns, clearly pleased with her catch. She tosses it in the air and eats it in only three bites. Then she shakes herself, sending water every which way and catching me off guard.

"Gwyn!" I laugh as I wipe water from my face.

"Sorry," she says sheepishly. "The fish make it worth it, but I don't love being all wet."

I stand and brush off my trousers. "Then let's keep moving. It's a sunny day, and I'm sure you'll be dry in no time."

Gwyn still needs to rest her wings, so we take the road that meanders through the lakes region. The path is well trod here, but we only pass a few houses and the outskirts of a village or two. Some places have patches of wildflowers, while others are squishy marshes that we avoid.

The going is slower than we'd hoped, but by the time night falls, we've reached the edge of the lake lands. Exhausted, we make camp quickly and then fall into a dreamless sleep.

༄

I am jolted awake in the middle of the night by Gwyn's squawking. My eyes fly open, but before I can take in the sight before me, rough arms yank me to my feet and hold me fast. Men have thrown a hood over Gwyn's head; she can't see, but the outline of her beak is working to peck through the fabric. Rope surrounds her paws and claws too, but if she can get her beak free, she'll make short work of those. Our packs have been upended, and our food and belongings are strewn over the ground as if someone was searching for something.

I gape as I recognize the man who stands by our fire glaring at me and glancing nervously at Gwyn. He's one of the men who chased us on the plains—and who attempted to take Cloud Castle from us. My breath leaves my body in a rush.

They've been following us.

And we, foolish as we are, made no attempt to cover our trail. Granted, we've moved faster than the men could, but we made no secret of how we've crisscrossed the continent for these treasures. Even if they lost our trail temporarily, it would have been easy to pick back up again.

The man folds his arms across his chest. "You've been tricky to find," he tells me. I swallow hard.

"Why would you be looking for us?" I ask more bravely than I feel.

My breath hitches again. Could they want revenge for driving them away from our castle?

"You claim that strange castle as your own, yet you abandoned it."

I try to straighten, but the person holding me doesn't loosen their grip. "Yes, we had...business that took us elsewhere."

The man narrows his eyes and stoops to my level, his nose only inches from mine. I do my best not to blink, but my heart throbs in my ears.

"Where did you hide the castle's treasure?" he asks.

I frown. "What treasure?"

He rises, shaking his head. "Every castle contains treasure. That's where they get their power. We've scoured every inch of that building, yet we've found nothing. Is that why you left? Did you take the treasure and hide it?"

"I have no idea what you're talking about," I tell him truthfully. But his expression makes it clear he does not believe me.

"Impossible." His eyes gleam. "We know you've been carrying jewels and silver with you. I bet you hid the gold first, didn't you?"

Confusion reigns in my head. "What are you—"

"Don't bother lying, we already found these." The man holds up the diamond in one hand, and another man behind him raises the chalice with a smirk.

"Those do not belong to you," I say, trying not to let my voice squeak. Though, in truth, they don't belong to me or Gwyn either. But at least we worked and faced challenges to obtain them.

"Ah," he says, eyes lighting up. "But they do belong to you and your castle, don't they?"

"No," I say. "We found them. We need them." I struggle yet again with my captor to no avail.

The man laughs. "Found them? I don't believe you. Trinkets like these aren't merely set out for one to come across."

Gwyn has been quiet since she heard my voice, instead focusing on the struggle with the burlap sack fastened over her head. She's almost through the burlap, and the men guarding her haven't noticed yet.

"We were sent in search of them. We need them to fulfill a bargain," I say carefully. I don't want these men to know the details, and I certainly don't want them to know we have one more treasure to obtain.

"Fine, don't tell us yet. But you will change your mind. We'll retrace your steps, and you will show us where you hid your treasure. Until you do, you're our captives."

"But our castle never had treasure!" I cry.

"It's pathetic that you think I'll believe a thing you say," he says. An awful grin spreads over his face. "If you refuse to show us where you hid it, your pet here could catch a fine price from those who keep such oddities in cages."

"Or dinner for days!" says one of the other men, sending laughter spinning through the group.

Horror shoots over me. I can feel the rage burning off Gwyn even though I can't see her face. She tears through the burlap, and before the men realize what's happening, she snips the ropes keeping her paws and claws in place.

Gwyn leaps forward roaring, knocking several of the men flat in the process. She charges at the man holding me fast, and he cries out, stumbling backward and releasing me. I grab the pack closest to me; then I swing up onto Gwyn's back as she runs. She takes off into the sky before any of the men can regain their footing.

Even as we fly away, I'm still shaking. Gwyn trembles under my hands, though it could be from fear or anger. Or both.

We've escaped, but the problem remains: We no longer have the chalice and the diamond. And most of our food was in the other pack.

"Gwyn, we have to go back. We need a plan, otherwise we'll never free the Wind," I say.

She growls in her throat. "If we return now, I will tear every single one of them apart. How dare they try to capture us! And steal from us!"

Her indignation is contagious, and now anger begins to take over me too. First they try to steal our castle, then our castle's supposed treasure, and then they steal the items we desperately need.

They must answer for it.

And we will make them.

CHAPTER 11

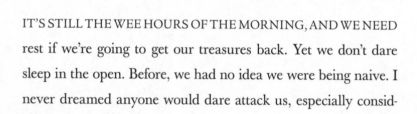

IT'S STILL THE WEE HOURS OF THE MORNING, AND WE NEED rest if we're going to get our treasures back. Yet we don't dare sleep in the open. Before, we had no idea we were being naive. I never dreamed anyone would dare attack us, especially considering how fearsome Gwyn appears.

Gwyn hasn't complained, but I can tell she's exhausted from only a small amount of rest. Her wings must be so sore. Several little villages and farms dot the landscape in the lakes region. An idea forms in my mind.

"Gwyn, we need to hide. Why don't we take shelter in the last place they'd look for us?"

Gwyn gives me the side-eye over her shoulder. "Where?"

"In one of these villages. Look," I say, pointing to a large barn on the edge of a farm. "I bet we could hide in that barn."

"Humans live on that farm. They're unpredictable and greedy. I do not like them much at all," Gwyn says.

"Yes, but that's where they keep the animals. We could rest there and make a plan to get the chalice and the diamond back with little likelihood of seeing any humans."

Gwyn lands near a clump of trees just outside the farm. Her eyes narrow. "I don't like this. It's too risky."

I shake my head vehemently. "It's even riskier to hide outside. Those men have been tracking us. They must know our habits by now, when we sleep, how long we can travel before we need to rest, and more. We have to do something unexpected, or they'll catch up to us again!"

"There must be a cave around here where we could sleep," Gwyn says. "I won't hide near humans!"

"We must!" I clap a hand over my mouth. I didn't mean to shout, but this is the first time I can recall arguing with Gwyn.

Gwyn snorts and claws at the ground. "You're going to wake every human within a mile!"

"Look, I'm going to stay in that barn. You should come with me," I say. Then I slide off her back and head straight for the barn, creeping through the field of grain between us.

"Aria!" Gwyn calls after me, but I ignore her. I'm positive the unexpected is the right move. The Wind's freedom, our lives, the world—everything is on the line. We can't afford to leave ourselves exposed again.

I reach the barn and sneak inside. Horses, cows, and a few goats slumber in various stalls. I spy a ladder leading to a loft filled with hay and carefully climb up. Moments later Gwyn enters the barn too.

"Up here!" I whisper loud enough for her to hear. A horse nickers softly nearby, but otherwise nothing stirs.

Gwyn flies up and lands beside me. Her feathers are still ruffled. "I'm not happy about this. But I can't leave you here alone either." She huffs.

"Let's get some sleep," I say. "When we wake up, we'll decide how to fight back."

We curl up in the hay, exhausted from our capture and flight. But we still sleep with one eye open.

First light arrives too soon and wakes us, along with the sound of animals eating. My stomach rumbles. The thieves stole our food too.

Another sound floats through the barn—humming.

My heart leaps into my throat, and I peek over the edge of the loft. Below us is a dark-haired woman cleaning a horse stall, singing to herself. The melody is very pretty.

Gwyn pulls me back so suddenly that I squeak.

"What are you doing, Aria?" she whispers. "That human might see you!" Gwyn's whole body quivers.

"I was listening," I whisper back.

"Who's there?" calls the woman below. She doesn't sound angry exactly. More curious but firm in tone.

"Now you've done it," whispers Gwyn. We move as far back in the loft as possible and hide behind a large bale of hay. My breath stutters in my chest. We've had enough trouble with humans already; I didn't intend to create more. But her song was so lovely...

The ladder creaks, and Gwyn's panic begins to rise. Her eyes bulge, and I can feel her heart racing as we huddle together.

"If someone's up here, come on out." The woman says. "I won't hurt you, I promise."

There's something oddly calming about her voice, but that doesn't quell the urge to flee. The floor creaks under her feet as she approaches our hiding place.

"I can't do it, Aria. I can't do it. I just can't." Gwyn whispers into my shoulder.

Before I can comfort her, she bursts out from behind the bale of hay and takes off, swooping down from the loft and right out the barn door. In the process, she knocks down the woman. And leaves me behind.

I gape after her. The Gwyn I know would never have abandoned me. I can hardly believe it.

But now the woman sees me as she gets back to her feet.

"Hello there." She dusts off her skirts. "Who might you be? And what on earth was that?"

Tentatively, I come out from behind the hay. "My name is Aria. That was my friend. I need to go after her." I try to go past the woman to the ladder, but she stops me, her brown eyes filled with concern and unexpected warmth.

"Hold on. What are you doing up here in my barn? Are you a runaway?"

I shake my head, thinking as quickly as I can how to tell her enough of the truth without revealing what I really am.

"My family was captured by someone awful. Then, on the road, all our supplies and...and"–what is the word humans use?– "money was stolen by thieves. We needed a place to sleep for the night."

The woman's eyes turn soft. "Well, I don't mind. I even have a spare bedroom if you need it. Just ask."

I smile. "My friend is an animal, so I think the barn is best for us. Thank you," I say.

She raises her eyebrows but lets it go. "Then at least let me feed you. Did those bandits take your food too?"

I nod. The woman shakes her head. "I know the sort. Horrible men. A group of them came through our village a few weeks ago too. You'll be safe here as long as you need."

"Thank you. You're very kind."

She smiles. "Name's Milly. Your friend's name is…?"

"Gwyn," I say. "I should go find her."

"What kind of animal is she? She took me by surprise, so I didn't get a good look."

I pause. I don't know this woman, but my gut says I can trust her. I swallow hard and hope my gut is right. "She's a gryphling."

Milly's eyes widen. "A gryphling? I've never heard of one around these parts before. Never seen one before either."

"I don't think many people have. She's very shy. Her kind usually keeps to the mountains and the sky."

"Does she like blueberry oatcakes? A batch will be coming out of the oven in just a few minutes."

"She'd love some, I'm sure."

Milly smiles. "Then I look forward to meeting her. I'll bring some out here for you both."

While Milly returns to the house up the hill from the barn, I set out in search of Gwyn. I'm still surprised she left like she did, but I feel guilty too. I knew this was pushing her comfort levels; perhaps I pushed too far. Her experiences with humans have been limited and traumatic. I should've known better, even though I still believe it was safest to hide in the barn. I find her in the shadows between the trees where we landed the night before. She's still shivering.

"Oh, Gwyn." I put my arms around her. "I'm sorry."

"I'm sorry too. I shouldn't have left you with the human."

"It's all right. Her name is Milly, and she's actually very nice. She's bringing us breakfast to the barn."

Gwyn sniffs. "Breakfast?"

"She made blueberry oatcakes."

She licks her lips. "I am rather hungry. I'm sure the barn animals are off-limits for eating."

"Definitely."

"Are you sure we can trust her?" Gwyn has mostly stopped shaking now.

"I think so. She's been nothing but kind."

"All right, I'll return to the barn with you. But we're leaving at the first sign of anything amiss. Agreed?"

"Agreed."

When we get back to the barn, Gwyn hides as Milly enters with breakfast.

"Sorry, Gwyn is very shy."

Milly nods understandingly. "Animals often are, especially around new folks. As much as I'd love to see a gryphling, I'll let you two eat in peace."

"Thank you," I say.

Once Milly is out of sight, Gwyn comes back down from the loft and sniffs one of the oatcakes. She snaps it up with her beak and eats it in one bite.

I laugh and eat one myself. They're warm and delicious.

"Now," I say. "How are we getting our treasures back?"

We spend the morning making plans. Gwyn will gather the local flying creatures to ask for their help. They can keep tabs on the thieves so we know exactly where to go and where they're keeping the treasures.

Then tomorrow, just before dawn, we'll take them unawares.

⟡

At first light, we head out, flying toward where the group of thieves have camped. According to a robin spy, the men were well into their cups last night celebrating their ill-gotten goods and are unlikely to wake anytime soon. That suits us fine.

The birds Gwyn enlisted fly ahead, reporting back that the men are still asleep. Soon we spy their camp from the air.

This time we're prepared.

We land a ways from the camp. Our bird friends saw no one keeping guard, and neither do we. The thieves may have mocked us for our lax precautions, but they are foolhardy too. On silent feet, we creep into the camp, ready to fly away at a moment's notice. How I miss floating more than ever! It would have given us the advantage we need. It might even have helped cover our tracks if my feet didn't have to touch the ground all the time.

Birds of all species and sizes perch in the trees that surround the men's camp. They are silent as sentinels. There are at least a dozen sleeping men, and I pick my way carefully through them as dawn gently rises over the lake nearby. Our second pack isn't far from the firepit, and I grab that and load it onto Gwyn's back first. Most of our food remains inside, to my relief. Then a flash of silver catches my eye—clutched in one man's arms. It's the same one who made the crack about Gwyn becoming their dinner.

I scowl as I bend down and gently disentangle the chalice from his grasp. He yawns and rolls over as I get it free. I still, not even daring to breathe for a whole minute before moving on. Our bird spies told us the diamond is in the leader's shirt pocket—and that the others called him *Russ*. He wouldn't let the diamond out of his sight. He's as entranced by it as I was. That might be trickier to get.

I tiptoe toward where Russ is asleep beneath a tree. Gwyn watches nervously nearby, while our bird friends wait to rush in and assist us if necessary. He lies on his side, his cloak tossed over him. I pull the cloak back slightly. His pocket is on the side closer to the ground. The outline of the large diamond rests over his heart. Crouching, I reach into his pocket as nimbly as I can and gently pull out the gem. Once I have it in my hand again, I let myself breathe.

We can still rescue the Wind.

I shove the diamond in my pack and run to Gwyn, only to trip over a root. The sound of my fall and the snap of the root resound in the camp.

The men begin to stir.

Panic sends me skittering back to my feet. I hardly remember swinging onto Gwyn's back and taking off, but as soon as we're in the air, relief begins to fill me. If only there were a cool breeze to calm the heat on my face and neck.

"That was too close," Gwyn grumbles as we fly over the remaining part of the lake lands. "I doubt they're done trying to get those treasures either."

I sigh. "I fear you're right. But this time we know they're out there, and we have the birds watching them. They can distract and throw them off our trail. When we get the Wind back, we won't have to worry about those men or set foot on this land ever again!"

Once, I might have enjoyed traveling, the novelty of it. At first it was nice to meet the otherlings. And Milly was very kind. But this experience has driven home how much I miss the Wind and my home in Cloud Castle.

But now we have what we need. There's only one more treasure left to liberate before our quest is complete.

CHAPTER 12

AS WE LEAVE THE LAKE LANDS BEHIND, WE'RE PRESENTED with the full majestic breadth of the volcanic range. We've seen it from high above in the clouds before, of course, but back then we were content to view it as simply part of the landscape passing below us. Now it feels very different.

Gwyn gawks, and a small whine wheezes from her throat as we approach. I can't help feeling like the air has suddenly grown thinner.

The range is massive.

The dark peaks stretch across the entire southern part of the continent as far as we can see in each direction. The Wind has told me the range is mostly dormant, but now that we intend to actually go into the mountains, it is very intimidating.

If we thought the coastline took a long time to search, then this is a rude awakening.

Some of the mountains are enormous, towering over the rest. Others are smaller, a few like foothills. Some have cratered tops, others maintain their craggy peaks. Woods cover much of them, and the highest peaks have snow sprinkled on their caps.

"How in the world are we going to find the right 'silent place' here?" Gwyn asks, echoing my thoughts.

My heart sinks. "I have no idea. I don't even know where to begin."

"I suppose we'll have to fly over them all to see if any clues stick out."

Gwyn soars toward the far edge of the range, and even that takes us a long time to reach. We circle each mountain and investigate several seemingly promising caves that go nowhere. Defeated, we finally set down in a lush green valley to eat and rest.

"I can't believe how little ground we've covered so far," I say. Gwyn snorts.

"This could take us days or even longer," Gwyn says.

The bread in my mouth tastes like dust. "You really think so?"

"If we want to be thorough, yes."

"We only have a day and a half left until the moon wanes. I

guess Worton really did set us up to fail, didn't he?" I set my food aside, no longer hungry. I gaze up at the vast array of mountains we have yet to explore. *Days* now sounds overly optimistic. Days we don't have. How long can the world survive—can we survive—without the Wind?

I leap up to my feet. "Look!" I point excitedly at the sky and the dark shadow flying over us.

Gwyn rises quickly too. "That's a dragon, I'd bet my life. They gravitate toward both fire and wind."

While we've been hesitant to reveal too much about what we're doing, it's become clear that we are unlikely to succeed in finding the elusive candle without some assistance. Maybe that dragon would be willing to help.

One glance and I can tell Gwyn is thinking the same thing I am. "Get on my back," she says.

We take off after the flying shadow. Gwyn is a swift flyer, but our quarry is faster. Try as we might, we can't catch up. We satisfy ourselves with simply following them. The dragon lands halfway up a mountain about a third of the way into the range and disappears into a cave.

Gwyn grows tenser as we near the peak. "Aria, I know you're accustomed to flying creatures of all sorts and sizes, but I think we need to be more cautious out here in the wild."

I frown. "Why?"

"We don't know this dragon, and we're about to approach them in their home, which dragons are notoriously protective of. We are not hosting them in Cloud Castle under the jurisdiction of the Wind. They may very well take one look at us and decide to gobble us both in a few bites. Or worse, roast us and save us for a midnight snack."

My stomach turns. I hadn't considered how much protection the Wind gave us in Cloud Castle. I have nothing but Gwyn to show that I'm a real windling.

But the truth is we're desperate. If we don't return to Worton with all three treasures before nightfall tomorrow, we'll never free the Wind. It's a risk we'll have to take.

"Then we'll be cautious and ready to flee at a moment's notice," I say, rubbing Gwyn's shoulder reassuringly.

When we reach the dragon's peak, Gwyn circles a few times before getting up the nerve to alight outside the cave. I remain on her back in case we need to flee quickly. The muscles in Gwyn's wings are strung as tightly as bowstrings.

"Hello?" I say tentatively. We wait, but there is no answer. "Hello?" I call again, louder this time.

From inside the cave, we hear something large moving, along with a rumble. I swallow hard, and Gwyn lets out a whimper. A growling dragon is not something anyone wants to meet face-to-face.

The sound grows louder, and then a puff of smoke greets us from the mouth of the cave. At first, alarm fills me, but when a familiar scaled snout pokes out from the shadow in the rock, I squeal with glee and slide off Gwyn's back.

"Neoma!" I cry. Neoma accidentally roasted one of our bird friends at the cloud castle, and we've only seen her once or twice since. Now that we're here, I realize I've missed her terribly. It's such a relief to see a friendly face.

"Aria?" The dragon's horned head appears in full, her heavy-lidded eyes blinking slowly. "Gwyn? What an unexpected surprise. I thought you never strayed far from Cloud Castle, but I haven't seen it in these parts recently."

I pat her snout in greeting, and she huffs again, the smoke tickling my nose. "That's why we're here, actually. The Wind is missing."

Neoma's eyes grow big. "Missing? How is that possible?"

Gwyn huffs and claws the dirt. I wring my hands and sit on a nearby rock. "Well, that's a rather long story–"

"Neoma, who are you talking to?" asks a voice from within the cave. I snap my mouth shut. Perhaps we won't be able to share the full story with our friend after all.

A girl appears in the cave's entrance, her arm possessively around Neoma's wing. Her hair is black as coal, but streaks of red and orange flames dance throughout it like the wind once did my own. Her eyes are a shocking blue. She frowns when she sees us. "Who are you?"

"Brigid, this is Aria, a windling, and Gwyn, a gryphling," Neoma says. "I know them from those times I visited the Wind in their cloud castle."

The girl sniffs. "I'm Brigid, a fireling. What are you doing all the way out here?"

I exchange a quick glance with Gwyn. While the rest of the otherlings were open and welcoming, Brigid does not seem at all happy to see us. In fact, if we didn't know Neoma, I suspect she'd tell us to leave her domain at once.

"We're...we're here to help the Wind. They've been taken captive."

Gwyn scoffs. "Well, not according to the man who has him. He claims the Wind is helping him, but he won't release them without something in return."

Brigid and Neoma gasp. "That's why the lull has lasted this long. I was beginning to wonder if the Wind had decided to slumber for a season. They did that once, but it was a long time ago and never since," Neoma says.

"How did the man manage to capture them?" Brigid asks. "Are the Fire, Earth, and Water at risk too?" Her brow furrows with concern.

Her question surprises me. I confess, I hadn't considered

that. Who knows what other tricks Worton has up his sleeves? But if we can do our part, he'll free the Wind. That's more than enough for us to worry about for the time being.

"I'm not sure," I say truthfully. "As far as we know, he only needs the Wind."

Brigid crosses her arms over her chest. "Well, that still doesn't explain why you're here."

Frustration begins to build in my gut. We're either going to have to tell her the whole truth or make up a lie. An idea strikes me.

"We came here to visit with Neoma. We thought she might be able to help us on our quest to free the Wind."

Brigid's arm winds around Neoma's wing again. I wonder if Neoma is her friend and companion in the same way Nixi and Gwyn are to Bay and me.

"All right, then. How can she help you?"

"Brigid," Neoma chides. "I think they wish to speak to me privately but are too polite to outright say so."

My cheeks flush. This is exactly what I was hoping.

"Fine, I'll go elsewhere." Brigid says, straightening. She looks to be about the same age as myself, but she is much taller. She stares directly at me. "Just be careful while you're traveling in the volcanic range. It can be dangerous, especially to newcomers."

I can't tell if the last bit is meant as a threat or a warning, but either way I'm relieved when she disappears back into the cave.

"Is there somewhere more private we can talk?" I ask Neoma. She bobs her huge head and slithers from the cave, leading us down a path to another opening. We follow her, and she curls her tail around her body as she settles onto a shiny pile of glassy black rocks. This must be her personal lair.

"How can I help you?" she asks.

"What we told you outside is all true," I say. "But there's more to the story than that. We're not sure who to trust; we only wanted to tell you." I glance nervously at the cave entrance. "I hope we didn't insult your friend."

Neoma laughs. "I wouldn't worry. She'll be all right."

"The man holding the Wind captive—he insists that the Wind is there of their own free will, but it's hard to believe."

Gwyn chirps. "You should have seen it, Neoma! The powerful Wind trapped in a huge glass orb."

A worried expression crosses Neoma's face. "That sounds terrible indeed."

"It was. But the man struck a deal with us. If we find three treasures and bring them back to him, he'll consider it a fair exchange and will set the Wind free."

"A quest," Neoma says.

"Exactly. We've managed to obtain two of the items. But we need one more, and we believe it is in the Fire's domain."

She raises one scaly eyebrow. "What is this item?"

"A candle that can penetrate any darkness and never burns out. According to the man, Worton, it 'burns bright in a silent place.' Might you have any idea where we should begin searching? This range is vast, and we must be quick. We only have until the moon wanes to return with the treasures. All we want to do is free the Wind and go home again."

Something glints in Neoma's eyes. Could it be recognition? I hardly dare to hope.

"Go home? Has something happened to Cloud Castle?" she asks.

"Why, yes, that's how we discovered something was amiss. One morning we woke up on the ground. Without the Wind to make it float, it's stuck there."

Neoma considers me carefully. "Aria, you no longer float either. I knew there was something different about you, but I couldn't quite put my finger on it."

"And her hair," Gwyn adds. "There's no wind rustling through it anymore."

"You poor creatures. You're right. We must do something. I believe I have heard of this candle. And the silent place…that rings a bell too."

"You'll help us?" I ask, eyes shining.

"Of course. Come with me. You'll need to fly on Gwyn to get there, Aria."

I get on Gwyn's back, and we take off. Neoma is a majestic creature, her wingspan engulfing Gwyn's. Her scales catch the sunlight, alternatingly appearing to be silver-blue one moment and reddish the next. She soars over the volcanic range with a grace no other creature can match as she swoops down toward a mountain in the very center.

Unlike the other peaks in the range that thrive with trees and life, this one is black and almost as shiny as the diamond that hides in my pack. It reminds me of the glassy black rocks in Neoma's lair.

"What is that?" I ask, calling out to Neoma.

"Dead Peak," she says. I shiver.

"That sounds ominous," Gwyn remarks.

Neoma circles, looking for a good place to land. As we fly over the mountaintop, I see it is not a full peak. Instead, there is a vast crater, making it appear as if the top of the mountain was once blown clean off by an eruption.

We land inside the crater. It's a wide bowl shape with a small raised area in the center. No vegetation grows here. No animals creep or skitter. It really is a silent place. The surface isn't as glassy or smooth as the side of the mountain. It has the appearance of tar-like substance that later hardened.

Neoma gestures to the lava tubes that dot the side of the volcanic bowl. "The tunnels lead to the magma chamber below our feet. It is the darkest, quietest place in all the lands. If the candle is anywhere, this would be it."

"The magma chamber?" Gwyn recoils. "Isn't that dangerous?"

Neoma shakes her head. "Long, long ago, yes it was. But this volcano is dead. It will not erupt ever again." She eyes another peak farther south. "The other mountains, however... Well, tread carefully is all I can say for certain. This place is not made for those such as yourselves. With the Wind to protect you, I'd never have worried, but now...I suggest you hurry about your task."

"Thank you for your help!" I throw my arms around Neoma's pretty, scaled neck. She pats my back with one of her front claws, careful not to pierce my cloak.

"Goodbye," Neoma says as she takes off. "I must rejoin Brigid, or she'll worry. I'm sure we'll meet again soon."

She takes off, no blast of air brushing our faces as she does so. A wave of sadness washes over me momentarily as I mourn the Wind's absence, but then I straighten my spine. We know what we need to do.

"Come on," I say to Gwyn. "Let's find that candle."

CHAPTER 13

WE VENTURE INTO THE CLOSEST LAVA TUBE. FROM WHAT Neoma said, it sounds like they all lead to the same place. We quickly discover the going is tricky and very slippery. In some places, the path slopes directly down.

I have no doubt we can get *down* to the candle. But I begin to worry whether we'll be able to get back out again.

"Aria," Gwyn whispers. "I don't like this place." She shivers as she hunches over as the passage narrows slightly. The only sound is that of shale shifting beneath our feet and our hearts throbbing in our chests.

I know what she means. It's pitch-black down here. I have a few matches in my pack, and we've been using them as slowly as we can. No glowing moss or fungus grows here to illuminate our path.

Nothing thrives down here.

"You haven't liked any of the places we've had to go to find these treasures," I say, trying to keep my voice from trembling.

"But this...this one is different."

A chill bursts over me. I wish the Wind were here. They have great power, and without them, I fear I am not a very good windling at all. But I can't afford to wallow, so I shove the feeling off. We have a mission. We must save the Wind.

We've walked for some time when suddenly I lose my footing. I drop the rest of my matches as I land hard on my bottom then slide, unable to stop, headlong down the lava tube.

"Aria!" Gwyn cries. In her hurry to follow, she slides too.

Terrified, I scrabble at the walls, desperate to find something I can hold on to or use to break my fall. Gwyn's claws and paws do the same, all to no avail.

I hit a bump and tumble head over heels. Finally, I manage to right myself but not slow to a stop.

We keep sliding and sliding and sliding.

My stomach is permanently lodged in my throat. It feels endless—then the earth rises to meet us without warning, and I roll, hard. I flop flat on my back on a field of ancient, solidified magma. Moments later, Gwyn thumps next to me in the most undignified landing I've ever seen.

Once our heads stop spinning, we see this space—huge as it is—is brighter than the tunnel we came down.

The source of that light is a burning candle set in the middle of the chamber. Unlike our other quests, there is no trick to figure out. I suppose the challenge is to get down here alive. Maybe to get out alive too.

After I get to my unsteady feet, I walk cautiously toward the burning flame. There might be hidden dangers I can't fathom yet. But I make it to the candle itself without incident.

I lift it with trembling hands. It's made from a deep yellow wax, set in a brass candlestick with a brass snuffer attached to the base. The flame is constant and gives off a pleasant warmth.

"I can't believe it. We found them all."

Gwyn chirps her approval then glances around nervously. There's no sign of danger, no one to swoop in and take this last treasure from us.

We really did it. Now we need to find a way out of here and deliver these prizes to Worton in exchange for the Wind.

I hold the candle aloft, illuminating the vast cavern. The rest of the floor is as glassy as this patch. More lava tubes mark the walls at random intervals.

Then the candle lights on something stark white. My stomach flips.

Bones.

We're not the first who've attempted to retrieve this candle. And by the looks of the dozen or more skeletons at the edges of the cavern and the fact the candle was still here for us to find, none have succeeded yet.

So this is why they call it Dead Peak.

I wish Neoma had thought to mention that, though she might not have known.

"Let's see if one of these other tubes will be easier to climb," I say to Gwyn, my mouth dry. We still have our packs with some food in case it takes longer to leave than we hoped. Those packs are lighter now, but it's better than nothing. Maybe if we yell loud enough, Neoma will hear us and come to our rescue.

I hope it doesn't come to that. Thus far, our unique natures have given us advantages these other questers have not had. I have to believe they will serve us well here too.

"Maybe one is wide enough for me to fly us out," Gwyn adds. That would be ideal. The faster we can leave here, the better. Then we could go straight to Worton. We might even be able to get the Wind back and Cloud Castle airborne within a couple days if we really hurry.

Hope fills me fast enough that, for a moment, I imagine I can float again.

The first tube we try is fine for a little, but then the steep incline becomes too much for us to handle, even with Gwyn's front claws. She might be able to claw her way out on her own—though with considerable difficulty—but definitely not with me on her back.

Disappointed, we move to the next one, hoping for better luck. But we're stopped by that incline only a foot from the entrance. We try the next and the next and the next, but in every single tube, we're met with the impassable problem of climbing up a chute that seems intent on keeping us trapped.

By the time we've tried all of them, real fear has taken hold of my heart. The bones that surround us may be harbingers of our own fate.

Gwyn begins to pace and hiss. I've never seen her this agitated before, not even when those thieves captured us.

"There must be another way out," I say, trying to calm her. Except her agitation is contagious.

We are creatures of the air. Being trapped underground is the worst fate either of us could dream up.

We had very close calls while retrieving the first two treasures. This time there might be no escape.

My pulse throbs in my throat as I try to calm my panicked thoughts.

An idea occurs to me. "We can't get out the way we came down. But maybe there's another direction we can go."

Gwyn moans. "Not down even farther!"

I shake my head. "No. Up." I point to the cavern over our heads. It's so high that we can't see where it ends.

Gwyn takes a deep breath then motions for me to get on her back. She takes off, and it feels good to be off the ground again, even if we are still trapped in a dead volcano. We fly the width of the ancient magma chamber with the candle held high, seeking anything that might indicate an alternate route.

In the center of the cavern ceiling, we find something: a wide vent, maybe twenty feet across, formed long ago by an eruption, that stretches upward as far as we can see with the candle's glow. With a nervous squawk, Gwyn flies into the vent.

The darkness looming around the edges of the candlelight still makes me uneasy, but hope makes me buoyant, balancing out the two extremes. We fly for what feels like a long time. Soon I begin to worry about my companion. The vent sides are smooth and have no ledges that might offer a place to rest.

"Are you all right, Gwyn? Should we head back down and take a break then try again?"

But my friend shakes her head vehemently. "I'm too anxious to rest. Finding a way out is the only solution."

With renewed vigor, Gwyn soars higher into the shaft. I'm grateful we found the candle, otherwise, nothing would light our way. I dropped my matches in the lava tube on the way down.

It isn't too much longer before the candle reveals we're

reaching the end of the line. A glassy black ceiling hangs above our heads. To my dismay, there is no sign of an egress leading outside.

However, the width of the vent has narrowed to about ten feet wide. Which, if I recall, is about the same width as the strange spoutlike thing we saw atop the volcano when we landed with Neoma. This must be it.

Gwyn squawks as she flaps her wings to keep us hovering. "All this way for nothing." She begins to descend, but I stop her.

"Wait," I say. "This still might provide a means of escape. Can you get me as close to the ceiling as possible?"

I don't have to see her face to know Gwyn's giving me a look, but she does as I ask. I put my hands up to the ceiling and feel around. It is smooth and cold. I push up. It almost feels as though something shifts. A small piece comes off and sails away to the floor far below us.

My breath catches. We need something harder than my hands. And more speed. Then we could use that shifting to our advantage.

"Gwyn, fly down a little then fly as fast as you can at the ceiling."

She cringes. "Really, Aria, that's dangerous. If I knock myself unconscious, we'll both fall to our deaths."

"No, it will work." I pull the diamond out of my pack. "The

ceiling shifted when I pushed on it. We can break through if we have more speed."

"We'll hurt ourselves!" she cries.

"No, we won't. We have the diamond. I'll hold it up over my head. It's the hardest substance in the world. If it can't break through, then nothing can."

"I'm not sure I like this…" Gwyn says.

"And I don't like us being stuck in a cavern for the rest of our lives," I say. I can feel her shudder under me.

"You're right. I like that least of all. We'll try your idea. It'd better work," she grumbles.

I hope it does too. Despite what I told Gwyn, I'm not certain it will. But this is the most promising avenue of escape we've seen, and neither of us has any better ideas on how to get out of this old volcano.

It's worth a try.

Gwyn descends for about a hundred feet. Then she circles once and shoots up with all her might toward the ceiling. Her wings beat faster and with more power than I've ever witnessed—a last gasp of energy made of desperation and fear.

We hurtle toward the ceiling, and I hold the diamond aloft in one palm, hoping it will be enough to set us free. I brace myself for impact and for the freefall that will come if we fail.

Gwyn screeches as we reach the ceiling, and I turn away, flinching. At first there's a moment of tension as the diamond meets the glassy black rock.

Then the ceiling shatters, raining rock all around us, and we burst free into the dying embers of daylight.

Pain shoots through my arm. I cry out and tumble from Gwyn's back as she struggles to find purchase on the lava field of the bowl. The diamond rolls out of my grasp, but it is unmarred from the task it just completed.

It truly is the hardest, purest rock in the world.

I cradle my arm to my chest, white-hot pain searing through me.

Broken.

That's the word that keeps running through my brain. I've never broken a bone before. Before, I could float; how could I possibly hit anything hard enough to break a bone?

I don't have the words to express how much this hurts.

Instead, I scream. Gwyn tries to calm me, the diamond and candle forgotten at my side. Faintly, I hear a familiar sound approaching through my own cries. It's comforting, but I can't quite place it.

"How do we fix this?" I manage to whisper to Gwyn through clenched teeth before another scream exits my mouth.

Neoma lands beside us. She assesses the situation quickly

by sniffing along my arm. I can't straighten it, and the pressure from her breath makes me scream again.

"You've shattered your hand and broken your arm in several places," Neoma says frowning at us. "What on earth were you two doing?"

"We'll explain later," Gwyn says curtly. "Can you help her?" She paces around us, clearly wanting to be of assistance but having even less of an idea how than I do.

Neoma nods her scaled head; then her rough tongue shoots out. I'm too surprised to move. At first, the touch of her tongue feels like fire then quickly cools, taking the pain with it.

Magic.

I've heard dragon saliva is a healing balm. I've heard it can even knit bones back together. I sit up, marveling at how much better my arm feels. It still looks awful, all bruised and bent, but there is no throbbing.

I give Neoma a curious glance. "Thank you, but—"

"Just give it a moment," she says with a slight smirk.

That's when the bones begin to shift inside my arm. It doesn't hurt, thanks to Neoma's magic, but it's a strange and uncomfortable feeling. I look away, and when the movement stops, I risk another glance. Aside from some remaining bruising, it's much better. I flex my fingers and bend my elbow.

Then I laugh and throw my arms around Neoma's neck. "Thank you, thank you so much," I whisper.

When I pull away, she notices the candle behind me, still burning, though it rests on its side. "You found it," she says, wonder edging her voice.

"We did, and then we couldn't find a way out. Those lava tubes are too steep. We couldn't climb back up, and there wasn't enough room for Gwyn to fly either."

Neoma hangs her head as understanding dawns. "I'm sorry," she says. "I didn't think of that. I should have gone with you. The lava tubes are no trouble for a dragon, but it should have occurred to me that it might cause difficulties for you two."

"Well, we had to get creative. We found the entrance to the old vent," I point to the outlet nearby, surrounded by shattered black glass. "Then we flew at it hard enough to break through."

Neoma blinks. "That is quite an unusual escape. And a harrowing one."

Gwyn squawks. "Yes, it was. You should have seen all the bones down there." She shivers.

I shiver too. "We were not the first to find the candle."

"But you will be the last," Neoma says. "When you return with the candle, I'll put it back where it belongs, and then I'll seal off these tubes with help from Brigid. We don't need any more people dying for this."

I retrieve our scattered possessions, putting the diamond back in my pack before I get too mesmerized by it and holding the candle in my hands.

"Will you be staying in the Fire region for a while?" Neoma asks. "We could have dinner together to celebrate your success."

Gwyn licks her lips. Neoma's idea of dinner is likely to be more in line with Gwyn's than Terran's was. But we have no time to waste. Tonight is the last night before the moon wanes completely.

"Not today, though we thank you for the offer," I say. Gwyn whines with disappointment. "Now that we have everything we need, we must free the Wind."

Neoma bobs her head. "I can appreciate that. When you return, then." We readily agree.

Our dragon friend waves goodbye as we take off in opposite directions. We fly west, straight for Worton's strange mansion to claim our lost parent.

A lightness fills me. We succeeded in our quest. We have won back the Wind. Soon all will be set right again.

CHAPTER 14

IT TAKES US A FULL DAY TO REACH WORTON'S DOMAIN.
Gwyn's endurance is pushed to the limits as we keep to the sky
as much as possible and only pause for food and rest when absolutely necessary. It is the only way to make it there before the
moon disappears. When the tall wall of briars comes into view,
I can't help but shudder. Gwyn tenses beneath me too. There's
something strangely foreboding about the briars that unsettles
us both.

Yet we have succeeded. We have the three items: the chalice that fills and empties on command, the candle that never
burns out, and a diamond of the purest form. The candle I've
had to hold in my hand, careful not to singe Gwyn's feathers or
fur, or myself for that matter, which has been tricky to navigate

while riding. But its light proved comforting when we camped last night.

It seems a shame to give these treasures to Worton, but we have no other choice.

It's for the Wind, and we will do anything necessary to free them.

Gwyn clears the briar wall easily, giving it a squawk of disdain as we pass over it. Then she lands on the front lawn. The first time we were here, we snuck in the back, but there's no need now. Worton is expecting us. We stride up the front steps and find the door unlocked.

"He really *has* been waiting for us," Gwyn muses.

The hall is empty and as fine and dusty as the parts of the mansion we glimpsed before. We make our way through winding halls toward the center of the building and the strange room with the metal dome—with the Wind trapped inside.

I open the door to the laboratory. My eyes automatically seek out the huge orb at the back of the machine. Between the confusing array of pipes and chutes, I can make out the Wind still swirling inside. My heart sticks in my throat. Worton sits with his back to us, hunched over a metal table, examining something so closely that he doesn't notice us until I tap him on the shoulder.

"Oh!" he says, whirling around. He wears a strange pair of

goggles, which he takes off and sets aside. A slow smile slides over his mouth as he recognizes us. "You again. Have you completed your quest? Just in time too."

His gaze is drawn to the candle I hold in one hand.

"We have." I grip the candle a little more tightly. "This is the candle that never burns out and can penetrate any darkness."

The wind swirls more violently in their glass cage.

Worton reaches for the candle. I flinch, instinctively drawing back. But I must give him this treasure and the others to free the Wind. I swallow hard and hold the candle out to him.

He takes it gingerly, almost reverently. "Beautiful," he whispers, seemingly to the candle. Then he addresses me with the glint of greed in his eyes. "Do you have the others?"

"We do." I take the diamond from my pack. Again, I feel an almost tangible repulsion as I place the gem in the palm of his hand. His fingers wrap around the diamond, and he clutches it to his chest.

"Perfect," he purrs as he stares at it. He moves back to his table and examines the diamond using a small contraption. "Yes, yes, yes. Absolutely perfect." Then he laughs and looks at me expectantly.

I pull the chalice from my pack as well. My hands quiver. There is something about his reaction that I do not like at all.

Gwyn huffs and scratches the floor next to me. The Wind swirls higher in their glass bubble. Are they eager to be free? Or are they trying to tell me something?

This time Worton doesn't wait for me to offer. He takes the chalice from my hand—a little roughly too.

"Ah, yes, even lovelier than I'd imagined," Worton says. He holds it up and says, "Fill." The chalice obeys, suddenly full to the brim with crystal clear water. My breath leaves my chest in a rush. So that's how it works. And how I must've accidentally called upon it as we tried to leave the sea cave.

"Well?" I say to Worton as he gleefully crows over his new-found treasures. He gives us a blank expression at first then begins to laugh. Gwyn and I frown, both disturbed by the strange man's behavior.

"We demand the Wind's release," I say, standing as tall as I can. It would be much easier if I could still float.

"You demand—you demand!" Worton howls with laughter. "Oh, you are too much. I didn't think you'd be able to pull this off, but now that you have, I have everything I need."

"Then release the Wind," I repeat. I cannot help but scowl.

Worton stops laughing. "Ah, but you see, I am not done with the Wind. Certainly not now that you have given me these trea-sures and the power they confer." He towers over me, but Gwyn steps forward, ready to peck at him should he try anything foolish. "These are mine, and so is the Wind. I will not give up anything, not when I have everything I ever wanted."

Horror rocks me, and I put a hand on Gwyn to keep myself from swaying. "You promised that if we brought you these things, you'd let the Wind go."

Worton shrugs. "I lied, obviously. And you believed me!" He shakes his head. "Truly, your gullibility is astonishing."

"You can't do that!" I cry, my hands balling into fists at my side. How I wish the Wind were free so they could blast this terrible man away with a huge, ice-cold gust.

"Of course I can. I hold all the power. And you, none."

Gwyn lunges for Worton, but I pull her back.

"Fools. If you hurt me, you'll never get the Wind back. I'm the only one who can operate this machine, and you must know its inner workings to get anything out of it. Magic holds it together. You may be able to harm me, but brute force won't release the Wind."

My heart quails. He's right; the machine is incredibly complex, a puzzle of parts I can't make heads nor tails of. And if the Wind is bound to it by magic...well, even the diamond probably couldn't free them from their glass cage. I frown at the machine. "What exactly does it do anyway? That you'd insist on holding the Wind captive?"

"It's an Alchemachine. Now that I have all it requires to run fully, it will transform any substance into gold. I can make my own wealth, make myself the richest man in the world. I can create money to give to the poor if I see fit, raise the stature of everyone I meet. With enough gold, I can do anything I please, and everyone will let me."

I shrink back. I've never had a need for money, though I've read about it in books the Wind has brought me, and I've watched people haggle in markets as we passed overhead. I knew the humans were fixated on gold, but this man is beyond obsession.

"You can't put a price on the Wind," I sputter.

"You're right. The Wind is priceless, and now they belong to me. Along with these." He runs his hands over the objects we delivered to him.

"If you're not going to hold up your end of the bargain, then give back those items!" exclaims Gwyn.

Worton shakes his head. "I don't believe I shall. But I will do you the courtesy of allowing you to leave this place unharmed, provided you do so immediately and never return."

Gwyn moves to lunge at him again, but I hold her back. This man is full of lies and trickery. I'm sure he's already prepared for the possibility of such an attack, and I don't want to find out what will happen to us in that case.

"Come on, Gwyn," I whisper to my friend. Gwyn whines but keeps her scowl firmly in place. We edge out of the room, never taking our stares off the man who betrayed us and the Wind. I gave him the benefit of the doubt before, but now I'm certain: the Wind didn't enter that machine willingly. Worton did something to trick them.

And somehow, some way, we need to get them out.

CHAPTER 15

THE DOOR TO THE LABORATORY HAS BARELY CLOSED before we hear other doors closing around us.

"Run, Gwyn," I say urgently. "Run!"

Doors appear along the hallway, sliding to block our path, but we make it through the first before it slams shut. We race down the hall to stay ahead of the others. When we reach the front door, I turn the knob and push with all my might, but it won't budge. I don't see any means of unlocking it either.

A terrible chill sweeps over me. "Gwyn, I think Worton lied about letting us leave too."

Gwyn screeches with anger. "What does he want with us?"

"I have no idea. Maybe he's just a terrible person. Who knows why humans do the things they do?"

"Well, we're not giving up. Get on my back. I'll fly our way out of here if I have to."

I climb on and hold her fur and feathers tightly. She takes off down the one open corridor, while the knot in my stomach tightens. Why is this hallway open? Are the slamming doors a random occurrence? I doubt Worton leaves much to chance.

Doors begin to slide out from the walls to block our path again, but Gwyn, fueled by rage and terror, manages to speed past them before they close on us. She turns down another hall, and I recognize she's headed out the way we first came in: through the back door. We're almost to the old kitchen when our path is blocked by another door. She takes a turn, flying right through a drawing room with all its furniture covered in sheets like sullen ghosts. We burst out on the other side.

The kitchen is right ahead of us now.

Gwyn lands at the back door. The handle is still broken. Worton either didn't bother to fix it or never realized we broke it. I throw the door wide, my chest filling with relief as Gwyn and I step through then carefully close it behind us.

If he doesn't know it's broken, that might work in our favor later.

Because I know, one way or another, we're coming back for the Wind.

We don't stop flying until we're well past the wall of briars protecting Worton's estate. When we finally stop to rest in a clearing, we're thoroughly exhausted. We eat a quick, cold dinner from our few remaining supplies and then promptly curl up together under a tree and fall asleep.

It isn't until the next morning that we notice something is amiss.

Our first trouble is trying to light a fire to toast bread for our breakfast. My matches were lost in Dead Peak, but the Wind once showed me how to use two rocks to create a spark. But this morning, no spark will come. I bang the rocks together over and over to no avail.

"We're probably too tired to do this right," Gwyn says. "Let's eat the bread cold. It's fine that way."

With a sigh, I'm forced to acknowledge she's right. It isn't worth exhausting myself over a simple fire we're only going to use for a little while anyway.

As we eat, we discuss what to do next.

"Should we return to Cloud Castle?" I wonder aloud.

Gwyn considers. "Perhaps. Or maybe we can ask some of our new friends for help with Worton and the Wind? They might have ideas on how to deal with him." Her eyes gleam wickedly for a moment. "I bet an encounter with Neoma would set him straight and make him give up the Wind. Or even one of the rocs, like Ria."

I laugh. "It might. Yes, let's see if Neoma can help us. I'm not sure where Ria is nesting nowadays, but Neoma is already aware of our quest, and we know where her lair is."

The rocs are enormous birds, the largest animals that fly. Ria has visited Cloud Castle many times, but not in the past few months. She could be making her home anywhere, and we haven't seen any sign of a roc's nest in our travels.

Gwyn is still exhausted from overexerting herself to get to Worton's estate in time, so we travel by foot in the direction of the volcanic range. This time we're on the lookout for ruffians like the ones we encountered a few days ago. Soon we're thirsty.

I drink the last of my water from my waterskin. "Gwyn, can you fly up to see where the nearest river lies? We should stop to refill our supplies."

She returns moments later with an odd expression on her face. "It's just north of us."

"What's wrong?" I ask.

"Well, it…it doesn't quite look right. Not like I remember it from when we passed here before."

The knot in my gut returns. A deep-seated certainty that all is not well in the land, and not only with the Wind.

"Show me."

As we approach the river, I can't help but notice the seasons appear to be changing early this year. It's still summer, but the leaves on the trees have begun to yellow. Some of the ferns that brush past my knees are starting to wilt.

When we reach the river, the bank looks more like a cliff. Before, the water rushed up to meet it; now, the river flows sluggishly and is at least a foot lower. Exposed tree roots hold the soil back as best they can, but parts of the bank are cracked and dried and look as if they slid into the river. Gwyn holds on to me while I fill my water supplies to ensure I don't fall in.

"I suppose it hasn't rained in a while," muses Gwyn.

"I suppose..." It's true, but could that really account for this? It hasn't been overly hot either, so the water drying up that quickly seems strange.

We follow the river for a while, curious to see if it deepens farther on. As we pass near a road that winds through the woods, we hear travelers. We take cover. It could be the thieves who tried to steal from us. Our bird friends haven't alerted us to their proximity, but it's possible they may have taken a new route or slipped by somehow.

Regardless, neither of us is in the mood to take risks.

We peek over the low bushes we hide behind. A family with a cart and horse trundles down the path. Snippets of their conversation reach our ears as they draw near.

"I will miss our home," the woman says wistfully, glancing behind them.

"Mama, will there be water where we're going?" the smallest child, a girl, asks. The mother swoops her up in her arms and carries her.

"I hope so, sweetheart. We've gathered as much as we can carry from the river, so we'll be all right until we find a place with a working well."

"And fires that work?"

The mother's face falters. My chest feels strangely tight and itchy. "That's the hope." She puts the child in the cart and exchanges a worried glance with her husband. He takes her hand and squeezes.

They move out of view, and Gwyn and I turn to each other. My heart beats in my chest hard enough that I can feel it in my ears.

"No working fires?" says Gwyn. "Wells that have dried up?"

"That's very odd," I say. "We had trouble setting a fire too."

"Could it be the missing Wind?" Gwyn wonders.

"I don't know. We had fire and water while we were on our quest to free them. But now..." I can't finish the sentence. I don't know what to say. I have no idea why these things are happening. But something truly strange is going on, that's for sure.

"Aria!" a familiar voice cries from behind us.

I turn to see Bay swimming up the river on Nixi's back. My

frown turns into a smile. Friends are a most welcome sight. "Bay, it's good to see you! What brings you here?"

Something about the waterling is different, though I can't quite put my finger on it. His expression is different too. Before, he seemed open and earnest, but today worry is written all over him, from his hunched posture to furrowed brows.

"We were hoping to find you, actually."

"You were?" I say, surprised.

"Yes, we thought you might be able to help. That maybe you had learned something." He pats Nixi on the shell as he dismounts to the riverbank.

"About what?" Gwyn asks, puzzled.

"The Wind, of course. Did you find them?"

"Yes, they're being held captive. But we failed to free them. We were looking for help too."

Bay's crestfallen expression at my words is striking. "Bay, what's wrong?" I ask.

"It's the Water," he says. "They're missing too."

CHAPTER 16

HORROR WASHES OVER ME. "THE WATER IS MISSING? WHAT happened?"

Now that I look closer at Bay, I see his hair isn't glossy wet like it was before.

Nixi yowls and rears on his hind legs, clacking his pincers together. Bay pats him, and the monstrous creature calms slightly.

"I don't know. Yesterday we went swimming, and I couldn't breathe underwater anymore."

"But you still have gills!"

"That's what makes it so strange. Nixi here went to Coral Castle in the deep to tell the Water something had happened to me. He found the castle empty. None of the fish there had seen them for at least a couple of days. It was like they simply vanished. I even tried calling the Water with my shell. This is the only time they haven't responded." He runs a hand through his strangely dry hair. "I guess some of my abilities must be magical, bestowed by the Water."

"Like my floating," I whisper. I hold on to Gwyn to steady myself. Bay's situation is all too familiar.

First my parent disappears and all the wind in the realm vanishes. Now the Water is missing too, and its elemental namesake is drying up.

An awful feeling comes over me. Fire isn't working anymore. And the trees…they're not changing colors early, they're dying. Same with the ferns and other plants.

And it all began yesterday.

The same day we gave those treasures to Worton.

One from near the ocean. One from deep under the earth. One from inside a volcano.

My fist clenches in Gwyn's fur, and she yelps. "Aria, what's the matter?"

Those weren't mere treasures; they were talismans, aligned with the elements. They must hold sway over them somehow.

That's how Worton did it. That's how he got the Wind to go inside his machine. There must be a talisman for the Wind too. Maybe he conned someone else into stealing it? Or maybe he did so himself?

However he obtained it, he now has control of all the elements. He's using their combined powers for himself, at the expense of the whole world.

Bay gives me a puzzled look. "Are you all right, Aria?"

Somehow I manage to find the words. "It's not only the Wind and the Water—it's the Fire and the Earth too. I'm willing to bet the others are missing as well. They're all in danger."

Gwyn shudders next to me as the same understanding makes its way through her. "We must warn the rest of the otherlings."

"You mean you've met an earthling and fireling too?" Bay asks, slightly awed.

"Yes, in our travels. The earthling, Terran, was kind and hospitable to us. But the fireling, Brigid, didn't seem to like us much." I bite my lip. She will like us even less when she hears the missing elements are our fault.

"Then we should waste no time. Where's the earthling?"

"In the deep woods. We can show you the way."

I get on Gwyn's back, and Bay glances back and forth between us and Nixi. He clearly doesn't want to leave his friend behind.

"Do you want to ride Nixi there? The river passes not far from the deep woods."

Bay looks relieved. "Yes, but I don't think he can go much farther than that. He can't survive out of water for long." Nixi rears and clicks his pincers together. "He needs to retreat to the ocean before the river dries up and he becomes trapped on land."

My breath hitches in my throat. Poor Nixi. And the poor trees too. They were Terran's friends. Worton's plan is having more dire consequences than I imagined.

Far greater than the loss of my own parent.

Guilt nibbles at the edges of my heart. This is our fault—mine, really. I should never have made that deal with Worton in the first place.

But I did, and now I have to fix it. Hopefully with all of us otherlings working together, we can get our parents back and prevent a disaster of epic proportions.

৩৯

We travel as quickly as we can, following the river to the deep woods. The trees look worse and worse as we go. Leaves decay, limbs are dried and cracked, and bark seems to be peeling off trunks. The ferns that once stood tall to my knees now wilt and brush the tops of my toes.

When Nixi can travel no farther, he stops at the riverbank, and Bay slides off his back. Nixi clicks forlornly, and Bay's eyes shine with tears. The waterling leans his forehead to the top of Nixi's giant shell.

"I'll miss you, friend. But don't worry, we're going to fix this. I promise."

A lump forms in my throat. What have we done? Can we even hope to keep that promise?

If not, once the rivers and lakes run dry, the ocean will dry up too. A vast number of creatures live there. They'll all die.

All because of my mistake.

These worries haunt me as we venture into the woods. We don't get far before we're found by Terran. But now, the green has leached from his hair, and his ability to hide in the trees is gone.

"Aria, Gwyn," he says in greeting. He looks almost sickly. I wonder if his connection to the Earth is affecting him physically as well.

"Terran, this is Bay. He's a waterling and our friend. We've come to warn you, but I fear you may already know the news we have to share."

"The Earth is missing," he says glumly. "Just up and vanished. One day they were here. The next they were gone. They keep to themself most of the time in their underground kingdom, but I could always feel their presence like a comforting blanket. I've been cold ever since the trees and plants began to wither." He rubs his arms seemingly without thinking about it.

"The Water has vanished too," Bay says.

"And the Fire," I add. "I haven't been able to start a fire since yesterday, and we overheard some human travelers talking about fire not working for them anymore either."

"What can we do? Where did they go?" Terran wonders. "Did you ever find a way to free the Wind?"

I grimace. "Not exactly. We thought we did, but...but it didn't work." I'm not ready yet to confess our accidental treachery. Besides, we need to get to Neoma and Brigid to warn them too.

"Now that we've found you, Terran, we must warn the fireling and one of our other friends, a dragon, that the Fire is gone." I frown. "Though they may have already noticed like you did. Regardless, having a creature as formidable as a dragon on our side will help us get them all back."

"You're friends with a dragon?" Terran gasps.

"We are. They're creatures of air and fire, and this one used to visit us from time to time at Cloud Castle. She's good friends with the fireling, Brigid."

"Then we should hurry. The sooner we can get our parents back, the better." Terran rubs his palm gently on a nearby tree, and some of the bark comes off in his hands. The sap beneath runs down the trunk like tears. I swallow hard.

"Agreed," Gwyn chirps. "I can take up to two of you, but I don't think I'm equal to carrying three."

"Then we have no choice but to walk," I say wistfully, though flying would accomplish our task much faster.

"Or you and Gwyn could fetch the others, and Terran and I can wait here for you?" Bay suggests. "The river where I left Nixi isn't far. That would give me a little more time with him."

"What's a Nixi?" Terran asks.

Bay grins. "My best friend. I'll introduce you."

"Good plan," I say. "That will be fastest. Last time it took us a couple days to travel there. We'll try to fly faster if we can."

"We can travel there directly, now that we know where Neoma lives," Gwyn says.

"Then we'll meet back here as soon as possible," Terran says. "Bay and I will do what we can to help the forest and the river in the meantime." Bay nods his agreement.

I get on Gwyn's back and wave goodbye to our companions. Then we take off, but I don't feel free and light like I usually do when we fly together.

A heavy weight fills me. We've only just made these new friends. I fear that when they discover the truth about what we did, we'll lose them. And the rest of the world will suffer for it too.

CHAPTER 17

GWYN FLIES FASTER THAN EVER, DESPITE MY WEIGHT. WE both feel the urgency of stopping Worton. We definitely need the others' help to do it. Especially Neoma. I hope she isn't angry when she discovers what happened to the candle.

I wish we'd never stolen any of those items.

We thought it was a simple quest. But those treasures were much more valuable than I'd imagined. I didn't want to know why Worton wanted them; I focused solely on freeing the Wind. Now the fate of the whole world rests on fixing my mistake: getting them out of Worton's hands and back where they belong.

We stop several times to rest. At one point, we spy Milly's barn and farmhouse and alight nearby. I'd hoped the blight hadn't reached this far, but the effects are clear here too. We see

Milly almost immediately, struggling to pump water from the farm's well. She pushes the lever over and over, sweat glistening on her brow, but it's no use. The well is already dry.

My stomach turns over.

"I don't think she'll want to see us right now," I whisper to Gwyn. She looks as nervous as I feel, and we quickly leave the farm behind, though the guilt trails us for miles.

It's been more taxing for Gwyn to fly ever since the Wind was stolen, but now the difficulty has doubled. Gwyn does her best, however, and we manage to make it to the edge of the lakes region before she must stop for the night. The abduction of the Water has impacted this region too. The lakes are definitely lower than they were a couple days ago. Water is disappearing at an alarming rate.

Our bird friends warn us the thieves are still in the area searching for us, and we're able to steer clear of the ruffians. We find a safe place to make camp, and when we wake, we eat a cold breakfast.

The food becomes ash in my mouth as the full impact of the Fire's absence hits home.

"People can't cook anymore," I say.

We're lucky we had plenty of food in Cloud Castle to bring with us and that Milly was kind enough to give us so many oat-cakes, though the lack of variety is beginning to wear on us. But it's a lot better than empty bellies. I glance at our thinning packs. It won't be long before we'll need to find a new source of food. Panic rises in my chest, but I shove it down as best I can.

We must fix this before we run out of food—or anybody else does.

Gwyn whines. "Aria, what did we do? I bear no love for humans, but I don't want them to starve. I don't want either of us to starve either."

Tears burn at the corners of my eyes. "I don't know. Worton tricked us. I should've given more thought to why he'd want those prizes, but I was desperate to get the Wind back. I didn't want to think about it. Now it's too late."

I put the remains of my bread and cheese in my pack, all hunger vanished. Only a terrible sick feeling remains in my gut.

We keep to the areas the birds tell us are safe, and soon we reach the edge of the volcanic range. It looks the same—aside from the wilting foliage—but something about it just *feels* different. Like it's darker and colder than before.

I shiver as Gwyn takes off and heads for the mountain where we found Neoma and Brigid. As we fly, I can't help but worry over the landscape as it passes below us. Then I spy a familiar shape on the ground.

"Gwyn!" I cry. "That's Neoma, and I think Brigid is on her back too."

Gwyn circles then lands near the dragon and the fireling. We're both breathless from relief.

"Aria, Gwyn, we set out this morning to find you. What brings you back here so soon?" asks Neoma.

I bite my lip. Brigid eyes me and Gwyn in a way that does not seem friendly at all.

"We came to warn you. The Wind is no longer the only one missing. The Earth, Water, and Fire have all disappeared too."

"Yes, we figured that out ourselves, thank you," Brigid says.

Neoma snorts a puff of smoke at Brigid. "That's why we wanted to find you. To see if you'd had any success freeing the Wind from that man, Worton?"

Part of me is frustrated that Neoma told Brigid about Worton, but that's what we're here to confess anyway. I suppose it doesn't matter much now. Not with all that's at stake.

"We failed." I stare at my feet. "Terribly."

"Now we need to band together to save the elements," Gwyn adds.

"We've already brought together a waterling and earthling. If all of us work together, maybe we can set them all free."

"Where are they?" Neoma asks.

Gwyn quickly gives her flying directions while Brigid sizes me up.

"Neoma told me you took a candle from Dead Peak right before the Fire disappeared. Does this Worton have it now?"

I can feel my cheeks redden. "Yes. Once we join the others, we'll explain everything that happened."

My stomach knots. There is no hiding our crime. We must come clean with them all to save the elements.

She eyes me suspiciously. I can almost see the wheels turning in her mind.

"Fine," Brigid finally says. "We'll come with you. Then you'd better answer all our questions."

Neoma ducks her head, and Brigid climbs on her back again. Then Neoma and Gwyn both take off. Neoma appears to be using an extra amount of effort to remain airborne like Gwyn. I wonder if the magic that made them both is elemental in nature and helped them fly. If so, Worton now owns that. But they soldier on, and we fly as quickly as their wings will take us back to the forest where we left Bay and Terran to fend off the decay on their own.

◦❦◦

When we land at the edge of the forest, we can see the river is lower than yesterday. It sudden feels harder to breathe. Like some looming weight presses down on me. I try to ignore it as Bay and Terran greet us, and we introduce them to Brigid and Neoma.

They are particularly fascinated by the latter.

Bay is nearly hypnotized by Neoma's blue-and-red iridescent scales. "Do you swim?" he asks her, and I can't help but laugh. I wouldn't be surprised if he had asked Terran the same question while we were off fetching the others.

Neoma smiles, showing her many rows of teeth. She means it good-naturedly, but Bay takes a step back. "Sometimes," she says. "I am creature of all the elements, not simply fire and air." She lets out a slight huff of steam. "But I prefer to stay warm, so I make the volcanic range my home. I admit, I prefer flying to swimming in general."

I hadn't realized dragons were of all the elements, but when Neoma says that, it does make sense. She lives in caves in the earth, can breathe fire, flies, and can use her sinewy body to propel through the water as well. I know of no other creature quite like dragons.

Brigid interrupts our conversation. "Well, we're together now. What can you tell us about the man who abducted the Wind, Aria?"

I swallow hard. This is the part I've been dreading. The part where I have no choice but to admit what I unwittingly did. My palms turn slick, and I wipe them on my tunic.

"The Wind was captured by a man named Worton. He lives in a decrepit mansion deep in the forest surrounded by a very tall and thick patch of briars. He has the Wind trapped inside a strange machine. They're stuck in this glass bubble, swirling aimlessly. At first, we tried to convince Worton to release the Wind, but he refused. He was adamant that the Wind had willingly gotten into his machine, but we could hardly believe it."

"We don't believe it at all now!" squawks Gwyn.

"No, we don't. We were persistent, and he made a deal with us: find and return with three legendary treasures, and he would release the Wind." I hang my head. "We were foolish to trust him. But we were desperate."

Brigid's mouth is a tight, hard line. "I know you were searching for a candle that never burns out in my region. What other items were you seeking?"

Terran speaks up. "You needed a diamond when I met you." He begins to look nervous. "Was that one of the treasures?"

"Yes, the purest and hardest diamond in existence. The candle, as you know. The third item was a chalice that fills on command."

Bay gasps. "You took the Water's chalice?"

I grimace. "Yes."

"But the chalice controls the flow of water around the whole realm. The oceans and rivers and lakes all stem from it." Bay's expression is one of horror. My hands fiddle with the edges of my cloak as I pull it more tightly around me. I wish I could curl up and hide inside of it so I didn't have to face my friends.

"I'm so sorry," I say. "We didn't realize what we were doing. We didn't understand the true significance of these treasures until it was much too late."

"What exactly is their significance?" Terran asks.

"They're talismans," Brigid says. "One for the Earth, one for the Fire, and one for the Water."

"Yes, and like fools, we brought them to Worton in exchange for the Wind."

Brigid snorts derisively. "Unbelievably foolish. Where is the Wind now? I haven't seen any change."

My chest tightens. "Worton refused to uphold his end of the bargain. The Wind is still his captive. We can only assume the Water, the Earth, and the Fire are now too."

"Worton must have gotten his hands on the Wind talisman in order to capture them like he did," Bay says.

"He must have, but I couldn't say how or even what it is."

Brigid begins to pace, while Terran's face is drawn. He slumps on a nearby log. Bay looks like he might cry.

"You stole our talismans and then gave them to this man who is using them to hold our parents captive?" Brigid says, folding her arms across her chest.

"Yes, and we must find a way to get them back. I thought Neoma might be helpful there."

Neoma, who has been quiet most of this time, huffs a bit of smoke. Her expression is unreadable, but I suspect she is none too happy with me and Gwyn.

"Perhaps, unless this Worton can control her with those talismans," Brigid says. A chill runs down my spine. I hadn't considered that. Indeed, he might be able to control all of us with the talismans if he wanted. If so, how can we hope to protect ourselves?

"Everything will wither and die," Terran says softly. "And we can't do anything about it."

"Well, we're going to try," Brigid says. "We need to decide on a plan and prepare well."

"Yes, we can all work together and—" I start.

Brigid laughs hoarsely. "You and your pet have done more than enough. Your selfishness may have destroyed everything!" She gestures to the dying forest surrounding us.

"It wasn't intentional. We—"

"That makes no difference! The damage is done." She stops and eyes me and Gwyn suspiciously. "We can't allow you to wreak any more havoc."

I take a step back. "What do you mean?"

"We"—she gestures to Terran, Bay, and Neoma—"will figure this out. You two can stay out of it."

"But we can help!"

Brigid stares daggers at me, but Bay sputters. "We don't need any more of your help!"

My breath hitches in my throat. I thought for sure Bay would take my side. But even he is angry at me.

Neoma steps between us. "It's late. We should all get some sleep. We can decide how to proceed in the morning. We're clearly not going to make any progress tonight."

"Fine," Brigid says. She stalks off to the other side of the clearing and begins to set up her bedroll. Neoma is right; it's gotten dark while we've been arguing.

Gwyn and I set up our own things on the opposite side of the clearing. It's hard to sleep with someone constantly glaring at you. I glance at Bay and Terran hopefully, but they won't even meet my eyes. That might feel worse than Brigid's glares. They join Brigid and talk in whispers without us. My stomach turns. I really liked these new friends, but it seems they hate me as much as Brigid does. Only Neoma gives us a pitying look.

I wonder if she feels a little guilty too. After all, she did help us find the candle.

"Let's all try to get some sleep," Neoma says. "Tomorrow, when it's light, I'll fly over this Worton's estate and see if I can glean anything useful. When I return, we can make plans to get the elemental rulers back."

We nod, and the otherlings grumble their agreement too. I settle down next to Gwyn, curling into her warmth, but it isn't as comforting as usual. I toss and turn for long enough that Gwyn begins to whine. Then, finally, I fall into a fitful sleep.

CHAPTER 18

WE WAKE IN A DIFFERENT LOCATION THAN WHERE WE fell asleep. At first it is startling, and I don't know what to make of it.

Then I realize tree roots are pulling me into the earth.

Panicked, I kick and flail, but I'm held fast. Gwyn's squawking draws my attention. She's in the same predicament, but the roots have pulled her halfway into the ground.

"Don't struggle," Terran says. "It will only make it worse. I'm sorry." He appears in the corner of my vision, but he won't meet my eyes.

Brigid comes up beside him and has no trouble staring me down. "We've been discussing it and have decided we don't trust you. We can't have you making the situation worse. This is the safest place for you two while the rest of us figure out how to get our parents back. Once that's settled, we'll set you free again."

"What if humans come by or, worse, a hungry predator?" Gwyn asks, a hint of panic in her voice.

"The trees will protect you," Terran assures us. "They're only here to keep you from joining us, not to harm you."

"But we can help!" I cry as the three otherlings step into the woods. Fear leeches into my bones. Every protector I've ever had has failed or disappeared. Now I can't even protect myself. I've never felt so helpless in my life.

The roots tug at me again. Despite what Terran says, I know they intend to pull me underground, where I'll be trapped like Gwyn.

I'm not going without a fight.

I scrabble for my pack before I'm pulled too far away. My hands close around the strap, and I clutch it to my chest. The roots are pulling my legs down, and soon my knees are covered by the dirt. Frantically, I search for the pocketknife I keep in the pack. When I grasp it, a hint of relief washes over me. I toss my pack aside, then slice at the root wrapping around my opposite hand. The root slithers away. I repeat the process with the roots holding my feet. I hold the knife to the one wrapped around my neck, and it almost seems to shiver. Soon the root releases and flees as if scared of me.

Breathless, I get to my feet and try to dig out Gwyn. But without a shovel, progress is frustratingly slow. Too soon, I'm exhausted from the effort. I sit next to what I can see of Gwyn in the dirt. I've barely made a dent.

"Gwyn, I'm so sorry," I say.

She shakes her head. "This isn't your fault. We tried to do something good, and it backfired. This"—she uses her beak to indicate her current situation—"is the others' decision, not yours."

"What are we going to do? I can't leave you here."

Gwyn looks at me earnestly. "You must. Escape without me so at least one of us is safe. If the otherlings won't let you help, maybe there's something at Cloud Castle that could be useful to the situation."

"I won't leave you," I say. "I can't do it."

"We're out of choices, Aria. Digging me out could take days."

"Days we don't have." Especially if the rate of decay in the forest and waters is any indication.

"Exactly."

"What will you do for food?"

Gwyn laughs. "I'll be still until something tasty dares to get close. Don't worry about that."

"I don't like this." I press my forehead to hers. "I don't like leaving you alone."

In truth I don't like being alone either. Even when I was alone in Cloud Castle, I was still surrounded by birds and knew the Wind would return the moment I wished them to by ringing my little bell.

My eyes begin to burn, and I squeeze them shut.

No, this is a very different sort of aloneness. One that makes me feel hollowed out inside and uncomfortable.

"Go," Gwyn whispers urgently. "Before they come back and realize you've escaped their trap."

"Gwyn…"

"Go!" She pushes me away with her head. That makes me take to my feet.

"I'll be back as soon as I can."

"Get out of here, Aria," she growls.

Finally, I do as she demands. But it feels like I'm leaving a piece of myself, the one part of my life that had remained unchanged despite all that happened, in the clearing behind me. Tears burn my eyes as I run through the woods, knife at the ready, desperate to get clear of the trees before any of them try to drag me into the earth again.

Except only dying, drooping limbs surround me. No roots grab me by the foot. When I break free of the forest, I drop to my knees to catch my breath.

Maybe I should be relieved, but more than anything, my

chest aches with despair. Everything has changed, and none of it for the better. I have no idea how to begin setting it right again.

CHAPTER 19

I WALK UNTIL MY FEET CAN'T MOVE ANY FARTHER AND THE sun has set; then I collapse near a dried-up pond. I remember passing it as Gwyn and I left Cloud Castle. Then, it had sparkled blue, and children from the nearby village had splashed in it. Now only a small pocket of water remains, surrounded by mud. The village is quiet and still, seemingly abandoned.

In the darkness the empty houses remind me of skeletal faces, mocking me and my failures. Numbly, I eat what's left of my bread and cheese, then curl up on my bedroll.

My last thought before sleep takes me away is that at least the stars still shine overhead.

☙ ❧

When I wake at dawn, my whole body aches from the previous day's flight from the forest. But I'm heartened to remember that the markers of the pond and the village indicate I'm not that far from the plains where the cloud castle lies.

A sudden burst of energy fuels me to pack up my meager belongings and get moving.

I need to see my home and know it's all right. If those men returned, I may need to get rid of them on my own. But one problem at a time for now.

I hurry through the fields and trees, trying not to notice how bad things are getting here. It was not long ago that Worton captured all the elements, but their captivity is truly taking a toll. I don't understand how he can value gold, of all things, over the lives of everything else.

When I reach Cloud Castle, I approach warily. I don't trust for one minute that those men won't be back. Without Gwyn, I can't communicate with our bird friends anymore, so I no longer know where they are. Nothing motivates the men more than the promise of treasure, and their ridiculous certainty that we're hiding some will no doubt prove too tempting to resist.

To my surprise, there's no sign of them here. It's quiet, save for the bird calls that are so familiar to me, I almost wish to cry. Cloud Castle, however, looks different. Gone are the lovely white cloud bricks that adorned the sides and turrets, leaving only wood behind. But I'm relieved it's still intact, even if the pieces once maintained by the Wind are gone. I keep low to the ground and hurry toward the back of the castle and the entrance to the aviary. I creep inside, and I'm met with a wave of birds of all shapes and sizes. All of them chirp and feed on the food stores we have for visitors. It's good the Wind keeps the cloud castle well stocked. At least half the food we had for the visiting birds is already gone. They flap their wings in greeting, and a few of the smaller ones hop onto my shoulders and nibble at my ears affectionately. I can't help but laugh. I may not have Gwyn with me, but at least I'm not wholly alone.

I haven't gone far when a great shadow appears from the back of the aviary, its wings tucked in tightly. My breath catches. "Ria!"

Ria the roc stands tall in the aviary, larger than any other creature here, far larger than Gwyn. Her size rivals Neoma's, but her wingspan is legendary. She's a formidable bird, and best of all, she's one of the few I can communicate with myself. Magical creatures are more accessible to me than regular birds, probably since I'm a creature of magic myself. Or at least I was until the Wind disappeared.

"Aria. Why is Cloud Castle on the ground? Where is the Wind?"

She puffs her feathers with concern, though to anyone who

doesn't know her, she'd appear ferocious. Now I understand why there are no humans near Cloud Castle.

One look at Ria and they would've fled for their lives. Rightly so. She could easily lift a full-grown horse in her talons. A man would stand no chance against her.

"The Wind has been captured. So have the Water, the Earth, and the Fire. A man has them trapped in a terrible machine." I shake my head. "It's all my fault. I was so desperate to get the Wind free that I made a deal I shouldn't have. Then the man wouldn't hold up his end of the bargain, and now everything is dying."

"Then what are you doing here?"

Her question feels like a slap, though I know it isn't meant that way.

"The otherlings—a waterling, an earthling, and a fireling—are angry with us. They don't want Gwyn and me to help since we messed up horribly the first time." I stare at my feet. To be fair, I can hardly blame them even though I don't appreciate their methods. "They trapped us, but I was able to get loose. Gwyn couldn't, and everything I tried failed. I came back here in the hopes of finding something that might be useful and keeping Cloud Castle safe from thieves."

Ria wears a satisfied expression. "Well, you don't need to worry about them again. Not for a while at least."

A wicked smile crosses my face. "You scared them off, didn't you?"

She tilts her head in assent. "It was my pleasure. When I realized the wind had died down and hadn't started up again for an unusually long time, I left my nest in the northern mountains to come here and find out why. I certainly never expected to find Cloud Castle grounded!"

"Neither did we. Gwyn was beside herself when we woke up here one morning."

"I imagine she was," Ria says. Poor Gwyn. She'll be sad to hear she missed seeing Ria. She has a lot in common with the rocs and loves to converse with them. "Whatever help I can offer you, Aria, please let me know. It's strange and unsettling without the Wind. Flying is more challenging too. If the other elements are gone too as you say, we'll all end up starving sooner or later." She shivers, which is quite a sight for a mighty roc.

I bow my head. "Thank you." She may indeed be a huge help. She'd certainly terrify Worton. But if I can't convince the others we need to all work together, what's the use? No, I need to figure that out first.

That will be the hardest part, of that I have no doubt.

CHAPTER 20

I'M HOME AGAIN, BUT IT FEELS ODDLY HEAVY. CLOUD
Castle was never meant to be on the ground. Maybe it's dying a
little too, like the trees and rivers.

I find food in the kitchen, though I'm surprised it's still here. I
thought for certain by now someone—humans or birds—would've
eaten it all. Regardless, I'm grateful for it.

After I eat a quick meal, I take comfort in the library. I miss
Gwyn, but I don't believe the otherlings will hurt her. They just
don't want her to interfere. While I'm angry at them for trapping
us like they did, I also can't blame them for it. If the situation
were reversed, I might feel the same way.

I run a finger over the shelves in the library as I examine the
spines and the knickknacks the Wind has brought me over the

years. Figurines, prettily carved boxes, and many unusual things too, like a spider trapped in amber and the skeleton of a petrified fish stuck in a rock from long ago. I've cherished all these things, as they've sparked my wonder and imagination. I've read most of the books in here too, some more than others. There are a few older cabinets in the library that I've only opened once or twice. Perhaps there is something in there that might help us thwart Worton's terrible scheme.

I dig through the first of several old cabinets, pulling out all manner of oddities, along with ancient books, even some scrolls written in languages I don't recognize. The Wind has traveled far and wide, after all. But after a while, I tire and take a break. I curl up in my second-favorite chair—my favorite was made of fluffy clouds and, like the sculptures in the front garden, dissipated with the Wind's absence—with a book of stories I found in one of the cabinets.

The cover is dusty and makes me sneeze, but the pages are filled with lovely illustrations and fascinating tales I've never heard before. I wonder why this book was hidden in the cabinet instead of placed on the shelves.

I read until my eyelids begin to droop. Then I begin a story toward the end of the book that makes me sit bolt upright. This one I recognize. It's the story Bay told us about the windling who wanted too much and eventually gave it all up.

Except in this version, the windling (and then waterling, earthling, and fireling) has a name.

Worton.

My head reels from the possibilities. Could the Worton who has caused so much damage be the same Worton from the story? The book is old enough that it feels like it should be impossible. Then again, otherlings like us do not age the same way as humans. Perhaps that was a gift the elements let him keep.

Which means Worton could be very old and have had a very long time to plot revenge against the Wind and the rest of the elemental rulers who couldn't give him the thing he desired most. It would explain so much. How he knew about the talismans and how he managed to get whatever the Wind's talisman was too.

I keep reading, unable to tear my eyes away from the page. When I reach the end, my breath stops short in my chest.

The Wind, the Earth, the Water, and the Fire were so sad to see him go that they crafted a key specially for him. He could use it to summon the elements if he was in need, and it would allow him to travel through their domains safely as long it was on his person.

I've seen this key. Worton wears it on a cord around his neck. I barely registered it at the time, but it's too much of a coincidence. The Wind's talisman must have been here in Cloud Castle, and no one can travel to the clouds safely except for a windling or a flying creature...or someone with that key.

Only the real Worton would know what the talisman is and where it was hidden.

I'm certain of the truth of this story. And of one other thing: I must tell the otherlings about this. It changes everything.

Because if Worton knew about the Wind's talisman, he must've known about the others too. It was only matter of time before he stole them all. He simply used me and Gwyn to speed up the process.

But it also means that we, as otherlings, are the only ones with any hope of defeating him. We must pool our knowledge— all of it—and use it to force him to relinquish the talismans.

I know just where to start.

I leap from my chair and hurry to the aviary, taking the book with me. To my relief, Ria is still here.

"Ria," I say. "I need your help."

The great roc caws and then bends down to listen to what I have to say. When I finish, I swear she is smiling as much as any bird can.

"I would be delighted to help you. When do we leave?"

"Tomorrow. We should all get a good night's sleep first. Then we can stock up on food and leave at first light."

With any luck, the sight of my new, larger companion—along with my new information—will be enough to convince the otherlings that we must act together. And we must be swift about it.

CHAPTER 21

THE NEXT MORNING, I PUT TOGETHER OUR SUPPLIES—
including the book with Worton's story—and then Ria flies us
toward where I left Gwyn. On our way, we pass the drying rivers
and the wilting forests. Humans wander out of their houses, beg-
ging everyone they see for any food they might have collected
before the elements vanished.

We also see the band of thieves. They're camped closer
to Cloud Castle than I'd like but not far from Worton's estate.
The first glimmer of an idea begins to form in my mind. If they
want treasure, maybe we should tempt them with it. Maybe they
can provide a distraction for us to get the talismans away from
Worton so we can free our parents.

But I first need to free Gwyn. I direct Ria to where I left her, and she wastes no time getting us there. Her enormous wingspan propels her faster through the air than Gwyn or Neoma, but I can still tell it takes a lot of effort without the Wind. When we set down in the forest, I close my eyes; Ria is cutting it close with her wings on the landing, and the last thing we need is a giant injured roc.

But she lands gracefully, and it only takes a few minutes to locate the tree where Gwyn is stuck.

She's sleeping when we arrive.

"Her head is above the ground, but the roots are holding her body fast below the earth," I tell Ria. The great roc merely shrugs then lifts one of her enormous, very sharp talons and scoops up the earth—gryphling, roots, and all. Her talons cut right through the roots like a knife through butter.

Of course, this wakes Gwyn. She flounders for a moment in the loose dirt, squawking until she sees us. Then her eyes widen.

"Ria! You're a sight for sore eyes," Gwyn chirps. Then she shakes off the dirt and gives me a big hug.

"I'm so glad you're safe," I say, burying my face in her neck feathers.

She harrumphs. "Me too. I don't think I'll ever trust trees again though."

Ria scoffs at the forest. "Just let them try that on me," she says with a warning tone. I swear a few of the livelier trees shiver.

"Have you seen the otherlings since I left?" I ask Gwyn.

She scowls. "Yes, they returned a few times to give me food. Which was nice of them, I admit. But they were none too happy you were gone."

"Did you hear anything of their plans?"

"They were still debating the best course of action. Neoma wants to simply burn the place down." Gwyn fluffs her feathers. "I rather like that idea myself, but I'm not sure Neoma has enough fire left in her to do it anymore."

"Even if she did, it might not work as well as she thinks," I say. "Worton isn't who we thought he was."

Her keen eyes regard me. "You found something in Cloud Castle, didn't you?"

"Yes, and we need to find the others and rethink our plans."

"What direction did they last travel?" Ria asks.

"Toward Worton's estate. They left not long ago. If we hurry, we can catch up to them."

I climb onto Ria's back again, and she and Gwyn take off. Out of the corner of my eye, I can see the band of thieves is now moving in the direction of Worton's estate.

We may be able to use that to our advantage.

But first we must convince the others to work with us.

We find them in a clearing about halfway to the briar wall. They had to walk instead of fly since Neoma can only carry one or two, so progress has been slow. Ria and I land behind Brigid, startling her. She gapes at the awesome creature. Gwyn lands nearby.

"Ria is here to help," I say. "So are we. We must work together, whether you like it or not."

"Why is that?" Brigid asks.

"Because Worton isn't who we thought he was. We assumed he was a greedy human. But he was once an otherling like us. In fact, he was all of us once."

Bay frowns. "But that's only possible in stories…"

"That's what I thought too. Until I found this version of your tale, Bay." I pull the book out of my pack. "It gives the boy a name: Worton. And it adds a new wrinkle. When he chose to give up his life as an otherling since he couldn't have all our powers at once, the Wind, the Earth, the Water, and the Fire made him a token to remember them: a key. Our Worton wears one around his neck–just as this story describes. Now, by stealing all the talismans, he's found a way to have all the elemental powers he desired. They must be one and the same person."

"Which means he won't be impressed by Neoma's fire," Brigid says.

"Not when he grew up knowing dragons and now controls the Fire."

"Then how are we supposed to defeat him?" Terran asks.

"We distract him," I say. "Use our wits to get the talismans back. Our knowledge of the elements should protect us from any tricks he might try, but not if it comes down to a fight with him."

"What can we use to distract him?" Bay asks.

I grin. "I have an idea."

We spend the rest of the day refining our plan, while our tiniest bird friends keep watch on the perimeter of our camp. We don't need anyone sneaking up on us.

We have no fire, though Brigid stubbornly tries to create one. Neoma tried first, but she can no longer breathe fire. She only coughs and a little smoke rolls off her tongue when she tries.

"I made a fire this morning," Neoma says sadly. "I didn't expect it to be my last."

Once we're all satisfied with our plans for the next day, we curl up, bedrolls not far apart, and fall asleep. Gwyn has an owl friend on the lookout at each of the four corners of our camp; they will alert us should anyone venture too close.

I stare at the stars for a little while, finding it difficult to sleep. Whether it's nerves or adrenaline, I'm not sure. All I know is that tomorrow either everything will be altered for the better, or this slow creep toward a dying world will be on a permanent, terrifying trajectory.

CHAPTER 22

RIA AND NEOMA FLY OFF THE NEXT MORNING ON THEIR separate missions. Here in the forest, Terran begins his own: finding trees still healthy enough to help us.

We slowly make our way toward Worton's estate while Terran talks to the trees on the way. Some are in worse shape than others. But a few here and there are willing to help us implement our plan.

Gwyn leads the way, and Bay hangs back with Terran, which leaves me to walk with Brigid. I can practically feel the fireling's dislike for me radiating off her in waves. I understand why she's angry, but if we want to succeed, her anger at me is going to be a distraction. I'm not entirely sure what to say to her. I've already tried to apologize multiple times to no avail. Nothing seems to make any headway with her.

Which is why I'm surprised when she begins a conversation with me.

"Bringing Ria was a good idea," Brigid says.

It takes me a moment to respond. "Thank you. I've known Ria for years. She visits the aviary in Cloud Castle at least once a year."

"She's bound to scare Worton out of his shoes," Brigid says. "Neoma too. But a dragon is a little less fearsome without the ability to breathe fire, don't you think?"

I grimace. Poor Neoma is distraught about this, even though she's tried not to let it show. "A little bit. But they have claws and teeth aplenty among them both."

Brigid laughs. "That they do." She goes quiet, but a few minutes later, she speaks again. "Now that the Fire has disappeared, I understand why you did what you did for the Wind. I don't approve of the stealing and how you went about it, mind you, but I can't say I wouldn't have done the same myself."

A tiny bit of relief fills me. Maybe we aren't destined to be enemies after all.

"It's a terrible, desperate feeling, isn't it?" I say. "The helplessness of not knowing what to do to save one's parent?" I shake my head. "It was very wrong of me. I should've realized what those talismans signified. I was distracted by my own fear and grief. All I could think of was that I'd do anything to save the Wind."

"Let us all hope it isn't too late to get the talismans back," Brigid says.

When we reach the wall of briars, we stop for lunch and to wait for Ria and Neoma to rejoin us. None of the otherlings have much food left, and I share what I brought with me from the cloud castle's food stores. Terran sits closest to the briar wall—one of the few things in the world not wilting—and appears to be communicating with it. He stops and touches a leaf now and then, smiling and nodding and generally seeming pleased with his unexpected new friend.

We're finishing up when the familiar beat of wings reaches us. Neoma flies toward us from the north and Ria from the south. They are not alone.

Two more dragons flank Neoma, their scales shimmering in the sunlight. Ria brings another roc and a hippogriff too. I shiver with hope. With more help like this, maybe we can do something about Worton.

We still must be careful. He knows more about all of us than we know about each other.

Our new friends land, and we make introductions. Ria introduces Reine the roc and Bryna the hippogriff. Gwyn is particularly delighted to make Bryna's acquaintance. Like Gwyn, Bryna is part bird but with the back end of a horse instead of a lion. They squawk at each other while Gwyn gets her up to speed on what's been happening. Reine the roc is as regal as Ria, but with pitch-black feathers and golden eyes. She bows her head at us in greeting.

Then Neoma introduces us all to Ismene and Ziska. While Neoma is a silvery blue with hints of red here and there, Ismene is a deep jade green with flecks of gold and blue, and Ziska is a sleek red and silver.

"Thank you all for joining us," I say.

"We could use all the help we can get," says Brigid, fondly petting Ismene and Ziska's giant horned heads in greeting.

"We knew something was wrong when the winds died and flying became more challenging," Ziska says. "But it wasn't until our ability to roast our dinner vanished that we became truly concerned."

"We will happily roast this Worton fellow for you if we get our fire back," Ismene growls.

"Only if I can peck out his eyes first," Bryna says.

"A deal." Ismene licks her lips.

I hold up my hands, tempted to laugh despite the gravity of the situation. "We must proceed cautiously. Worton was once a windling who became a waterling, then an earthling, and then a fireling. Now he has control of all the elemental talismans."

"And he'll definitely use them against us," Bay says.

"His mansion is full of tricks too. Gwyn and I barely escaped the last time. This won't be a simple matter of doing away with him."

Terran clears his throat. "I have an idea," he says. We all turn to him expectantly, and his cheeks redden. "I've been talking to the briar here." He points to the enormous wall of thorns nearby. "They're healthy because Worton has been keeping them safe, but without rain, they know they will eventually wilt and die. They grew to their current stature due to magic Worton wielded, but they don't like him any more than we do. They want to help."

Reine steps forward. "Can they move?"

"When they wish to, yes." Terran glances at the briars again. I swear I can hear them rustling. "I'd say they're very motivated."

"Then perhaps they should be the advance guard. They could tighten their ring around the mansion and prevent Worton from escaping if he tries to flee," Reine says.

"After they let us through," Brigid adds.

Ria and the other flying creatures all nod their agreement. Terran smiles. "I'll tell them."

"There's another resource nearby that we can use to our advantage, especially if the wall of thorns will open to let certain people and creatures through," I say. "A band of human thieves is nearby. The birds have been keeping tabs on them for us because they tried to steal the talismans while we were collecting them. They've been searching for us ever since."

Neoma tilts her head at me. "How would we use them exactly?"

I grin. "All we have to do is tell them where the treasure is now. Their arrival will distract Worton, and pitting them against each other will leave a path open for us to take back the talismans."

"We won't actually let them have the talismans though, right?" Bay asks.

Brigid scoffs. "Definitely not."

Gwyn huffs. "The humans will be much easier to scare than Worton."

Ismene smiles, showing her enormous and very sharp teeth. "Then let's get to it."

We divide up our tasks then set our plan in motion. Terran explains the plan to the briars, and the wall begins to come down. It's quite a sight to behold. The prickling vines slither toward the ground and then creep forward, their white roots snaking along with them. We let them encroach on the estate before we approach. Then Gwyn and I take off to find the thieving humans.

They're easy to locate. The birds point us in the right direction, and we simply follow the sound of arguing. We startle them when Gwyn bursts over the trees and lands in their path. When they regain their bearings, their leader steps forward warily.

"Did you change your mind? Come to share the treasure with us after all?" The men behind him laugh.

"No," I say bluntly. "Someone cannier than you stole the treasure from us. But you might be able to steal it from him."

His eyes narrow. "What do you get out of this? Why should we trust you?"

"He isn't worthy. We'd rather have the treasure in human hands than his."

"And where is this treasure now?"

I point in the direction of Worton's estate. "There's a mansion, grand but crumbling. The man who lives inside hoards many strange and valuable things. You might even find something of more value than our simple treasures if you search hard enough."

"Thank you for the tip, girl. We'll discuss whether this is a trick and will perhaps check out that estate." He tries to be coy, but I can see the glint in his eyes. The same glint that shone in them when Gwyn and I were captured and he was ranting about treasure.

They'll come to the mansion, of that I have no doubt. And my friends and I will be ready and waiting.

◌০৩৩

We let the briars do their work first. Their creeping is slow but steady, and when they surround the mansion, we make our first move. The door to the old kitchen in the back of the estate is still broken. Worton must not know about it. Or he does and doesn't care because he's focused on the power he holds now.

But it serves our purpose, and we otherlings cautiously enter through the kitchen. Gwyn and the rocs and dragons and hippogriff wait to make their appearance. We intend to be sneaky at first to escape Worton's notice. But if that fails, our flying friends will provide a distraction.

We must find those talismans so we can liberate our parents.

Bay wrinkles his nose at all the dust in the kitchen. "Is this how most humans live? It hasn't been cleaned in ages. Where I come from, the water always keeps everything clean."

"It's the closest thing I've seen to a human kitchen, but I hope it's not representative of all of them." Milly's barn looked cleaner than this place does; I'm sure her kitchen was clean too.

"If he's the only one here, it shouldn't be hard to find what we need," Brigid says.

"There's a good chance what we need is never let out of Worton's sight," I say, and the others sigh heavily.

We tiptoe into the hall. We decided to split into pairs to search the estate and confirm the items aren't somewhere other than the lab; then we'll regroup here and enter the lab together. Brigid and Terran will search the east wing, while Bay and I take the western side. Gwyn and I saw some of the estate the last time we were here, but we didn't have time to look around in our urgent escape.

Now we get the chance to explore.

And hopefully not get caught in the process.

We pass faded tapestries and paintings that adorn the walls and try not to step on the creaky parts of the floor. The first doorway we peek into reveals a large ballroom with a dusty black-and-white tiled floor and walls that must have once been polished mahogany. Fine chairs and sofas with faded red velvet cushions line the walls, and gauzy curtains do little to keep the light out of the place.

But there's nowhere to hide the talismans here as far as we can see, so we move along quickly. The next room was once a dining hall; inside is a table with carved legs that are beginning to rot. The table wobbles when Bay bumps into it accidentally. We search the cabinet in the dining room, but all we find is old silver, fine dishes, and half-used candles. None of them resemble the special candle we need to free the Fire.

Disappointed, we return to the hall and move on to the next room. And the one after that, and after that, and after that.

Not one of them is any kind of treasure room. Even the library contains only dusty books, and not one cabinet is filled with oddities.

I'm nearly positive Worton has all the talismans with him. He will not relinquish them easily.

Bay and I leave the last room at the end of the west wing empty-handed and head back to our meeting place to wait for Brigid and Terran.

When we reach the kitchen, Brigid and Terran are nowhere in sight. Bay glances around nervously. "Do you think they're all right?" he asks.

Their absence makes me nervous too. But I put on a brave face for Bay. "Maybe they had more rooms to search. Maybe they even found something."

"What if they were caught?"

I put a hand on his shoulder. "Then we'll rescue them too."

I peek into the kitchen to see if they're hiding in there. They might have ducked inside if they saw Worton roaming the halls. But all I see is the same old kitchen and the first tendrils of the creeping briar making its way inside.

Before I can investigate the kitchen more thoroughly, a door closes sharply down the east hall. Bay and I hide behind the kitchen door. But no heavy feet fall on the floor. Curious, I peek around the doorframe. Worton, with tiny flames rolling over his damp-looking hair, slides from the hallway into another room— but he isn't walking, he's floating.

Shock rolls over me. He's *floating*. He took *my* power, *my* gift from the Wind. I'm willing to bet he can also breathe underwater, blend in with plants, and do whatever it is Brigid used to do too.

He's made himself into what he always wanted to be, commands the beauty and wonder of all the elements. But even that isn't enough. His thirst for power of all kinds now includes the human greed for money and gold.

There's a frighteningly good chance we'll be no match for him, even with our large and terrifying friends. Moments after Worton disappears into the other room, Brigid and Terran sneak down the hall, coming toward us as quickly and quietly as they can, looking rattled. We all hurry to hide in the kitchen, shutting the door gently and ducking so he can't see us through the glass panel in the door.

"What happened? What did you find?" I ask Brigid and Terran.

"We nearly ran right into Worton when we tried to leave our last room. It was a bedroom, and we hid under the bed until he left." Their eyes are wide as saucers.

"Did you get a good look at him?" I ask.

"A little," Brigid says.

Terran seems like he's about to explode. "He was camouflaged when he first entered the room. He took my gift from the Earth."

My jaw sets grimly. "I know. He can float too, just like I used to. He has everything he ever wanted." I take a deep breath. "He's made himself into the ultimate otherling."

CHAPTER 23

"THEN FIRE CAN'T HURT HIM NOW," BRIGID SAYS. SO THAT'S the fireling's gift.

The briars surround us in the kitchen, but they leave us alone at Terran's direction. There's only one thing left to do before we go to the lab.

"I'll signal Gwyn, and then we search the lab. Keep watch in case he changes rooms," I say. We need to be quick to take advantage of Worton being out of the room.

I get to my feet and creep outside, then give a loud whistle. The beat of wings greets me in return. Gwyn lands in front of me, the others following close behind.

"It's time," I say. "If we're not out in ten minutes, come in after us."

The beasts share a grim look and give their agreement. When I return to the kitchen, the others are ready and waiting.

"He hasn't left the other room yet," Brigid reports, closing the door where she'd stationed herself.

"Good. Hopefully whatever he's doing in there will take a while and buy us some time," I say.

We sneak into the hall. The door to the strange lab isn't that far, but it feels like it takes an eternity for us all to reach it. Brigid gets there first and pulls open the door gently, but it still squeaks, echoing loudly in the corridor.

Worton must not hear it. He doesn't burst from the room he's in, and we hear nothing from that direction at all.

With our hearts in our throats, we enter the lab.

Shocked gasps ring out beside me as the otherlings take in Worton's massive machine. In fact, I think it might be even bigger than when I last saw it. Three new glass orbs protrude from it. One contains a wild mass of ivy and dirt, another is filled to the brim with water, and the last glows with firelight.

Each orb holds an elemental ruler. One of our parents. Panic slides up my throat, but I can't let it overwhelm me.

We must find those talismans and set them all free.

Bay approaches the orb containing the Water, eyes glistening with tears. He places a hand on the outside. The water swirls in recognition.

"They know we're here," he whispers.

Terran and Brigid greet their parents similarly but with more anger than sadness.

"Where do you think he's hiding the talismans?" Terran asks me. I point to the numerous cabinets lining the walls.

"My best guess is there or in one of the worktables." There are several tables and old desks Worton uses as workstations around the room. One of them holds the huge book I've seen him poring over. I draw closer to examine it while the others ransack the cabinets. The pages are thin yet somehow not brittle. The markings on the pages are strange to me. In some places I can make out letters I recognize and some words but nothing to render this grimoire intelligible. He must've spent ages studying to be able to read it, let alone build a machine such as this to harness the power promised in the book.

Stymied by the unreadable book, I search the drawers in the table. There are many papers and some objects too, mostly plain rocks. But before I can go much further, Bay gasps. I whirl around. He stands in front of an open cabinet. It's filled with gold. Not bars or coins, but the raw kind humans mine from the earth that glitters despite being buried in the dirt.

If the rest of these cabinets are similarly full, Worton has enough raw gold to have emptied an entire mine.

I glance back at the drawer full of gray rocks. That must be what he needs these for. To put into his Alchemachine and turn them into gold.

"What does he want all this for?" Terran asks, wrinkling his nose.

"Money and the power that comes with it," I say. "At least that's what he told me." I gesture to the drawer open before me. "I think he must put these plain rocks into the machine, and they come out like that."

"He's destroying our world for money?" Brigid says, her face reddening with anger and frustration. "But that makes no sense!"

I don't disagree. "I know, believe me. But somehow it makes sense to him." I shake my head.

"Humans are very strange creatures," Bay says.

We resume our search, and I move on to another table. This time the drawers are locked. Hope flutters inside my chest. Frantically, I search for something I can use to break it open, alighting on a hammer. It looks heavy enough to smash the locking mechanism into the drawer. I strike at the metal lock—once, twice, three times. On the third try, I'm rewarded by a satisfying crunch, and the lock clatters to the floor. I yank open the drawer, and a familiar sound greets me: the tinkle of wind chimes.

There, inside the drawer, are the wind chimes that always rang out in Cloud Castle. I'd know them anywhere. They stopped the night the Wind disappeared. I woke up because I wasn't accustomed to the silence. I'd completely forgotten about that until now.

The chimes must be the Wind's talisman. Though how Worton managed to get himself up to Cloud Castle and steal them is still a mystery.

I pick up the chimes reverently, and as I do, I feel a breeze brushing past my face and rustling my hair. Then a stronger gust and an almost ticklish feeling runs up my arms. I never felt that with the other talismans, but I'm a windling, and this belongs to me and the Wind.

I whirl around and hold up the chimes. "Look!" I say, a little louder than I intended.

"Is that the Wind's talisman?" Bay asks.

I nod excitedly. "We should check the rest of these drawers to see if yours are here too."

The others draw closer, and Brigid raises her eyebrows at me. "You're floating," she says.

She's right. My feet no longer touch the ground. Now that the chimes are in my possession, the gifts of the Wind are returning to me. I feel lighter inside too, more than I have in weeks.

Brigid takes up the hammer next and smashes into the remaining locked drawers. I run toward the Wind's glass bubble, wondering how I'm supposed to use this to free them. Worton used it to trap them, but was it intuitive or through a spell from his grimoire? Since he was once all four otherling types, he probably had the same reaction as I did to each of the talismans.

I'm steps from the Wind's orb when I hear two cries: one of joy and triumph, quickly followed by one of fear. I shove the chimes into my pack so I don't drop them and hurry toward the others. At the edge of the machine, I halt in my tracks. Worton has caught Brigid by the throat. The ever-burning candle lays on the floor, the snuffer over the top to keep the flame contained. Terran and Bay throw themselves at Worton. I move to join them but draw back when Worton whispers something, sparking a huge flame in their direction.

Bay cries out in pain, clutching his arm to his body. My hands close into fists even as shock jolts through me. The talismans don't just give Worton control over the elemental rulers but over the elements themselves. He can use them against us.

Bay and Terran retreat, and I stay hidden. If Worton doesn't realize I'm here, maybe I can use that surprise to help them. I'm no help if I'm captured.

"How did you three get in here?" Worton narrows his eyes at Brigid while she chokes and kicks at him. "You're otherlings, aren't you?" He laughs and tosses Brigid aside. She slides across the floor before slamming into a desk. She shakily gets back to her feet, rubbing her neck.

"You came here to steal back your talismans, didn't you?"

He shakes his head. "No need to bother. You're no match for me with all the elements under my control." He turns up his palm, and a flame dances on it for a moment. "No one can challenge me now."

"No one can truly control the Water!" Bay cries.

"Nor the Fire!" says Brigid.

Terran simply scowls at Worton.

"On the contrary," Worton says. "I can and I do. They will obey me and bring me everything I want. They already are." His smile vanishes. "Now leave my home while you still can."

He gathers the talisman on the floor and retrieves the chalice and the diamond from one of the other destroyed drawers. When he turns toward another of his desks, Brigid, Bay, and Terran can stand it no longer—they all throw themselves at Worton. Brigid attempts to wrestle the candle from his grasp, while Terran yanks at the arm that holds the diamond. Bay clings to the chalice, but Worton raises his arms, and a blast of wind catapults the otherlings off him.

"Like I said, you are no match for me."

Fear rushes through me. Even though I now hold the chimes, Worton still has the power of the Wind. It must be because they're still his captive. I must figure out how to release the Wind from the orb and from his control.

And fast.

Before Worton can return to his work, Ria, along with Gwyn and the other flying creatures, burst through the door to the laboratory. The room is huge, and the ceilings are high, making it possible for them to fly here. Ria catches him in her claws, but she only has a hold on him for a moment before she screeches with pain and drops him on the floor. He must have used fire on her feet. I can smell singed feathers from where I hide.

The dragons take him on next, diving for him one by one, but he beats them back every time. First with water, then fire, and finally vines that grow out of nowhere and pluck Neoma from the air, pinning her to the ground.

The flying creatures screech at him from the air as he approaches Neoma. She angrily huffs smoke in his direction. He laughs.

"You're a fine prize too. I could put you into the machine and make a ton of gold out of you."

"Don't you dare!" yells Brigid. She and the otherlings have gotten to their feet but hang back to stay out of the flying creatures' way.

"Now, this is a fine place," says a familiar voice. Russ, the leader of the band of thieves, strides into the laboratory flanked by his men.

At their arrival, Worton almost seems nervous. We and the monsters rely on the elements for our power and to fight. The humans have man-made weapons Worton cannot control or warp.

Worton steps forward. "You're trespassing. Leave now—or pay the price."

Russ chuckles. "I don't think so. You see, you have something we want. Something we've been searching for. Treasure. We've earned it. You only stole it."

The men begin to argue, and I take advantage of this distraction to hurry toward the Wind's orb. If I'm going to figure this out, it's now or never. The Wind swirls when I approach and place a hand on the glass.

"How do I free you?" I whisper.

The Wind doesn't answer, but they make a familiar noise. The first few notes of my favorite lullaby. The Wind last sang it to me before they were caught up in Worton's net. I wonder if the Wind sang the same song to Worton when he was a windling. Usually I find it comforting, but now it only makes me sad.

I pull out the chimes, holding them up to the glass. "Come out," I say, hoping it might allow the Wind to leave of their own volition. But the Wind simply swirls and swirls.

I press the chimes to the glass this time. "Let the Wind go free," I command. But again, nothing happens. Frustration builds inside me. The talismans enable Worton to command the elements; there must be a way for me to do so as well.

An awful thought occurs to me. What if I need the grimoire–that I can't decipher–to do this? If that's the case, then the Wind and the other elemental rulers may be permanently trapped.

Tears burn the corners of my eyes, and I lean my back against the orb, sliding down the side until I'm sitting on the floor. This isn't going to work. We're going to fail and our whole world will die and fade away–including us otherlings. Only Worton and his gold will be left.

The Wind hums a few bars of the lullaby again, and this time the chimes tinkle in response. I sit up straighter. They haven't chimed at all since Worton took control of them, even when I put them in my bag. But the lullaby provoked a response. I scramble to my feet and turn to the Wind.

I'm certain my parent is trying to tell me something. Now I think I understand what it is.

I hold up the chimes and begin to hum the lullaby I know so well. I don't do the song the same justice as the Wind, but it's a fair rendition. The glass orb seems to waver in front of me. Before I can finish the song, the entire Alchemachine is rocked, knocking into me and sending me and the chimes flying. They slide off into a corner.

While I get my bearings, the men struggle with Worton for the talismans, and the flying creatures have joined the fray. One of them must have knocked into the Alchemachine. I scramble to retrieve the chimes then sneak over to the otherlings. They're huddled together whispering.

"There you are, Aria," Terran says.

"Sorry, I was trying to free the Wind," I say.

"We saw. We're going to make a play for the talismans while Worton is distracted by the others," Bay says to me. "Glad you still have yours at least." He eyes the chimes in my hands.

"Did you make any headway freeing the Wind?" Brigid asks.

I frown. "I'm not sure. Maybe. I need to keep trying."

"Why don't you do that, while we go for talismans?" Terran suggests. "If you can get the Wind free, that would be the best distraction of all."

We all agree and head off in different directions.

With the only talisman we've liberated, I hurry back to where the Wind is held prisoner. Between the twisting metal tubes of the machine, I spy the first hints of the briar creeping in through the doorway. They must have followed the flying creatures' lead. Worton doesn't appear to notice it yet, but he may soon.

I can't help smiling. That ought to catch him off guard.

Hopefully Terran can get the diamond back before the briars attack Worton.

I must hurry to free the Wind and give him the distraction he needs.

When I reach the orb, the Wind immediately hums the first

bars of the lullaby. With hope tight in my chest, I hum them too and every bar after until the end of the song, all while pressing the chimes to their glass cage.

I feel something not only stirring within me but beside me too. A faint breeze.

Then it's as if a lock has been released. The Wind rushes through the tubes and whirls into the air above the Alchemachine. My heart soars with them. They whisk around me in a silent thank-you then fly to the other side of the machine where Worton and the thieves argue. I follow suit. Some of the thieves have begun to pocket the gold from one of the cabinets. Much to Worton's frustration, the creatures block him from stopping them, and the Wind now rushes around him with all the righteous fury of a cyclone. Worton's eyes widen when he sees me.

"You again? I should've known you'd rile up the others and cause trouble."

"More trouble than you think," I say, unable to hide my smile.

He starts toward me, but a tendril of briar catches him by the ankle, sending him tumbling to the floor. The diamond rolls out of his hand, and Terran swoops in to pick it up before clutching it to his chest. Russ and his thieves draw back toward one corner, gaping at the slithering briars.

Confusion reigns on Worton's face, and he struggles to

get to his feet, but another huge gust of wind forces him to remain prone.

That is, until the briar wraps around him completely, pinning his arms to his sides and his feet together, and lifts him off the ground. Worton struggles to hold on to the remaining talismans, but the Wind strengthens the gust until the candle and chalice clatter to the floor. Brigid and Bay waste no time retrieving them. Even though the Earth isn't free yet, now that the diamond is no longer in Worton's possession, the briars move a little faster than before. Like some power was holding them back but is now gone.

The briars crawl over Worton's entire body, even filling his mouth and preventing him from shouting. They lift him up, up, up and over the Alchemachine until he's poised above the funnel at the top. His eyes are wild, and he struggles, but it's to no avail. The briars' hold is too strong.

Then they let him go.

He falls into the funnel, arms flailing, and the machine begins to churn. The Wind wooshes back into the glass orb, but this time I can tell they chose to. The elements in the machine swirl, and strange lights and noises fill the air. There's a terrible scream. Bay clutches my arm, and I clutch his too.

I'm not quite sure what's happening. All I know is that I wouldn't want to be in Worton's shoes.

Finally, the Alchemachine stills. Something slides down the central chute and clanks as it hits a large bucket.

We all draw closer, curiosity winning out.

Inside the bucket is a huge heap of raw, gleaming gold.

CHAPTER 24

WITH WORTON DESTROYED, THE SPELL KEEPING THE
Earth, the Water, and the Fire trapped in the machine is broken.
The elemental rulers, free at last, reunite with their children.

The Wind envelops me in a warm, breezy embrace. "Aria,
my child. I always knew you were brave, but I never expected
you'd be called upon to prove it in such a manner." Gwyn joins
us too and is similarly welcomed by the Wind.

"We need you," I say. "The world needs you too." After a
moment, I can't help but ask the question that's been bothering
me. "Why didn't you ever tell me about Worton?"

Indeed, until I read about him, I never had given much
thought to whether there had been any windlings before me.
Now I want to know more.

The Wind's sigh brushes across my cheeks apologetically. "Worton was a painful subject. He was once very dear to me. I should have told you."

"Were there other windlings too?"

"Yes, long ago. But none who ever behaved as Worton did."

"Can you tell me about them?"

"When we get home, I will tell you about each and every one of them," the Wind promises.

I smile, pleased. No more secrets.

I glance at the otherlings. The Fire greets Brigid and Neoma, taking the form of a huge burning flame but without singeing the floor. They flicker around the girl and the dragon, and Brigid grins broadly for the first time since I've met her. The Water forms a wave, sliding across the floor toward Bay. He runs to greet them, and the wave curls around him, hiding him from view momentarily. The Earth takes the form of a large blooming vine and wraps around Terran, who leans into the affectionate gesture.

All of us reunited at last.

But we have one last issue to deal with: the human thieves.

The men drew back when the briars attacked Worton, and now they stand in one corner of the room. The leader, Russ, appears both nervous and angry. He catches my eye and steps forward.

"What about us? You promised us treasure," he demands, scowling. All four of the elemental rulers in their various forms move protectively in front of us otherlings. Russ takes a step back.

But I push forward. I'm no longer afraid of these men. We have more power than we believed.

"Take the gold from the cabinets for your villages. Divide the wealth evenly between everyone. We'll know if you don't. We'll be watching."

Russ doesn't seem completely happy with that answer, but the rest of the thieves don't hesitate to fill their bags and pockets with the remaining gold and make a hasty retreat from the estate. Russ is the last to leave. But leave they do.

It's a strange sight to see all four elemental rulers in one single place, but they greet each other like old friends.

Bay approaches me with a bashful expression. "Aria, I'm sorry I was so angry with you before. We shouldn't have tried to stop you from helping."

"You had every right to be angry," I say. "I should've come to you for help as soon as we left Worton's. You knew the significance of the chalice, and had we understood that, everything might have been different." I hang my head. "Instead, I ignored my gut feeling that something wasn't right about the quest he gave me and Gwyn. I didn't allow myself to see any further than what I needed to do to free the Wind. I was willfully ignorant. I'm sorry."

"Me too," says Gwyn, clawing at the stone floor.

"Next time, come to us first, all right?" Bay says.

"Hopefully there won't be a next time," Gwyn says.

"But if there is, you can count on it," I say.

"And you can count on me," Bay says.

Terran and Brigid nod their agreement. "Us too," Brigid says.

This journey has brought me far from home and widened my understanding of the world. Before, I was content to watch the world pass by below me. The people and places seemed more like dolls than real living things with wants and needs and feelings. It was easy to forget that, safe in my castle in the clouds.

I will never take that for granted again.

"Let's go home," I say. The otherlings beside me cheer.

The elemental rulers bow to each other, and we leave the mansion—this time through the front door. Then the Wind takes to the sky, the Fire flickers along, the Earth creeps, and the Water flows, all of them back to their domains. The otherlings each get on the back of a flying creature so they can reach their destination quickly. We're all eager to return to our lives and heal the damage Worton has done.

All of us, that is, except the briars. They spread into the

mansion, winding through the halls. This is their home now. They've claimed it so no one else can ever be tempted by the Alchemachine or Worton's grimoire.

Gwyn leaps into the sky with me on her back. This time, a breeze tugs at my hair and cools my face. A thrill ripples through me. I've missed this so much that it feels like my heart could burst with relief. I can tell Gwyn relishes it too.

We wave goodbye to our new friends and go our separate ways, and soon Gwyn and I reach Cloud Castle. The Wind is waiting for us. The trampled cloud blossoms are beginning to bud again, and the sculptures in the garden have mended themselves. The Wind curls into a smile when we land beside them; then they blow an enormous gust toward the castle.

Cloud Castle begins to rise. Slowly at first, then gaining speed. I let out a cry of joy, and Gwyn takes off again, racing the castle to its rightful place in the clouds. When it finally settles in the sky, all three of us enter the castle together, home at last.

ACKNOWLEDGMENTS

It's hard to believe that *A Breath of Mischief* is my tenth published book. It's the seventh book with my brilliant editor, Annie Berger, and my sixth with Sourcebooks Young Readers. I'm so grateful to have found such a wonderful home for my stories, and so lucky to have such talented people to work with. Here's hoping there will be many more tales to tell together in the coming years.

As always, I must thank my indefatigable agent, Suzie Townsend, her current and former assistants Dani Segelbaum, Sophia Ramos, and Kendra Coet, as well as the fabulous staff at New Leaf Literary and Media. You make the magic possible!

Special thanks to the rest of the Sourcebooks team who works tirelessly behind the scenes to make my books shine and get them in the hands of readers, in particular, Annette Pollert-Morgan,

Heather Moore, Chelsey Moler Ford, Jenny Lopez, Ashlyn Keil, and Margaret Coffee (and no doubt many, many more!).

I must also profusely thank the cover artist, Yuta Onoda, for bringing Aria and Gwyn to life so beautifully! The artwork is stunning, and so perfectly captures the characters.

Finally, love to my husband and sons, Jason, Logan, and Xavier. Thanks for all the mischief!

ABOUT THE AUTHOR

© Kristin Hardwick

MarcyKate Connolly is a *New York Times* bestselling children's book author who lives in New England with her family. She graduated from Hampshire College (a magical place where they don't give you grades), where she wrote an opera sequel to Hamlet as the equivalent of senior thesis. It was also there that she first fell in love with plotting and has been dreaming up new ways to make life difficult for her characters ever since. You can visit her online at www.marcykate.com.